CROSSOVER

BY

John C. Dalglish

2013

Dear Reader,

Before you embark on what I hope will be an enjoyable journey, I wanted to address an issue that has presented itself in the early reviews of this book.

I am a Christian. I believe in the plan of salvation and the infallibility of the Word of God. In writing this work, I have attempted to remain true to the character and love of our Lord.

Having said that, I must tell you this book is written for pure enjoyment and fun. The concept of Chasers and Runners is purely a fiction of my mind, and a vehicle for the story.

It is not my desire to put forth any suggestion of this being a reality of the Spirit world.

It is fantasy and fun.

So please enjoy, and rest assured that my only goal was to entertain without any of the junk the world puts in its books.

God Bless, John

CHAPTER 1

The dull ache in the back of my head was fast becoming a pounding that made its way towards my temples. As I began to come around, I moved my head back and forth, forcing the cobwebs to clear. When things came into focus, I recognized my surroundings. My office in downtown St. Louis, exactly where I was going when everything went black.

I tried to sit up, but found myself tied to my rolling desk chair. Whoever tied me up, also rolled me over in front of the window on the south wall. Normally, the old leather chair would sit behind the desk on my right.

The office door, complete with distorted glass and the words 'Jack Carter Investigations', was directly ahead of me. The bathroom is to my left, which despite my current predicament, I felt the need to use right now. My day always starts, continues, and finishes with lots of coffee. Also, there's a bottle of Tylenol in the cabinet, which my head was crying out for.

To say that I found myself in an unusual situation would be somewhat disingenuous. In the seven years I'd been a private investigator, I've been kicked, punched, cursed at, and even spit on. However, being tied up was a new one for me. What added to the novelty of my current state was I didn't know who was responsible.

In past altercations, I always knew who was taking their best shot at me and why. Husbands I'd exposed cheating on their spouses, disability claimants who were surprisingly nimble when not at a doctor's office, and even a woman who told her husband she was 'working out', while going to a different sort of club with her girlfriends.

But currently, my caseload was light and, as far as I knew, my enemies were few. It was then I heard a voice; not just any voice, but a booming, throne room of God, rattles your insides, type voice. If I wasn't tied in the chair, I might have fallen out of it.

"Jack Carter, hear what I say or you will die."

Okay, not the first thing you expect to hear when you think God is talking to you.

"Is that you, Lord?"

"I am not your lord!"

The voice and its source, moved around in front of me where I could see it. Seeing him removed all doubt as to whether his voice came from God. In fact, the speaker looked like the guy at the opposite end of the 'good versus evil' spectrum.

My office is not large, but when this deep voice behemoth moved around in front of me, the space suddenly became claustrophobic. Six foot four or five, shaved bald, with grey eyes that appeared to shimmer. His body seemed to be square, almost as thick as it was wide, but all muscle. A full-length black trench coat, black t-shirt, and black boots increased the incredibly ominous look.

"Who are you then?" I asked.

"Who is not important, but why I am here is. I have come to give you a message."

"Was it necessary to hit me in the back of the head, then tie me up, to deliver this message?"

I get sarcastic when I'm terrified. Actually, I'm sarcastic most of the time, just more so when I'm scared.

He ignored the comment, which was probably good for my health, and the shimmering gray eyes bore down on me, forcing me to meet his stare.

"This is a warning. You will receive a call to service and it will be up to you to choose your path."

"Well good, because I like to make my own decisions." I have to learn to shut up.

"Do not mock the opportunity I am giving you!"

I held my tongue.

"You can reject the call and live. If you accept the call, I will be forced to kill you."

I was about to object to the killing part when he looked over his shoulder towards the door, back at me, and disappeared. Gone. There one second and not there the next. My head really hurt now.

I looked behind me, but he wasn't there. Bending over as far as I could, I looked under my desk. My head spun and I sat back up.

Idiot! That guy could barely get his knees under your desk, never mind hide there.

I tried pulling at the ropes again but nothing doing. I would have to wait for someone to show up. Fortunately, the wait was short.

The door to the office crept open slowly, and an elderly man peered around the edge. He was clearly trying to be stealthy, but when he saw no one besides me in the room, he relaxed and entered.

As he shut the door behind him, I couldn't help but think of Yoda from Star Wars.

'*Here to save you, I am.*'

Short, with just a ring of gray hair, he wore a flowing white robe that went all the way to the floor. When he turned towards me, the robe was open in front, and I could see a leather belt surrounding his waist, blue jeans, and a blue t-shirt. In his hand, he carried a wooden knife or short sword, which he put into the belt as he walked up to me. A wooden cross, too big for his chest, hung around his neck.

"Are you okay?"

"My head hurts but I'll survive. You came along at just the right time."

"Actually no. If my timing was right, I would have been here before he hit you over the head and tied you up."

I found that logic hard to argue with. He undid the ropes and I rubbed my wrists as I stood up.

"You know the guy who did this?"

"I do. I've been tracking and chasing him for nearly thirty years."

"Thirty years? Some sort of personal vendetta or something?"

He moved around the office, checking the bathroom before going to the window.

"No, not a vendetta. A calling."

There was that word again. 'Calling'. I could see I was clearly out of the loop on something here.

"What kind of calling?"

He turned and looked at me.

"A spiritual calling. A mission from our Lord."

"Our Lord? You know who I call Lord?"

"Yes; Jesus Christ."

Okay, so that was an easy one. I'd given my life to Christ when I was in college, some twelve years ago. Since then, I'd always worn a silver cross around my neck. I reached down to see if it was showing and found it gone. I looked around the chair but it must have been lost when that goon hit me over the head.

"Your cross was not lost. Your attacker tore it from you because of his hatred for the symbols of our Lord."

Okay, this day had now turned full-fledged creepy. I rolled my chair back over behind the desk and sat down. He watched me but didn't move from the window. I stared back at him, studying him, which didn't seem to bother him at all.

"What's your name?"

"Buddy Daniels."

"How do you know these things about me?"

"I can't tell you."

I should have known. "Why not?"

"Well, let me restate that. I can't tell you, *yet*."

"What about that thug, can you tell me what his name is?"

"He calls himself Harbinger; his real name is Steve Mason."

"Why are you chasing this Harbinger guy and why does he call himself that?"

"Can't tell you that yet, either."

"What *can* you tell me?"

He looked directly into my eyes now.

"Only that you are about to receive a calling on your life that will change your path; *if* you accept it."

"Are you here to bring this 'calling'?"

"No, I can't call anyone to this mission. Only God can place the call, and the gifts that go with it, on your life."

"So this calling is what 'Big and Black' was warning me about?"

"It is, but you mustn't let him change the path for you. You must make the choice based on your own values, and the direction you decide is right for your life."

All of this cloak and dagger was making my head hurt worse, and I remembered the Tylenol in the medicine cabinet, which also reminded me I still needed to pee. I got up and walked around my desk towards the bathroom. Yoda watched me with serious eyes and I felt the need to explain myself.

"I need to use the bathroom."

He just nodded at me and turned back towards the window. At least he wasn't going to follow me.

I closed the door and relieved myself. When I was done, I opened the medicine cabinet and retrieved the bottle of painkillers, washing three of them down with a glass of water. I looked at myself in the mirror.

I'd looked worse but couldn't remember when. Raccoon circles had started to form around my hazel eyes, and I could feel some blood matted in my light brown hair. While I'm not a big guy, just a shade over six feet, I had taken a pretty good blow, and lived to tell about it. My YMCA gym membership must be paying off.

Bending over, I splashed some cold water on my face, and went out to see if I could pry any more information out of Yoda. The office was empty.

For all I knew, he'd done the vanishing thing like 'Big and Black', but there was no point in worrying about it. I needed to lie down, and taking the rest of the day off seemed just the tonic for what ailed me.

I locked up the office and went down the stairs, I don't trust elevators, and found my car where I'd left it.

My car is actually not a car. A 1978 Ford Ranchero, it's a sort of hybrid car-truck thing that serves both purposes. Its color and its current state can best described as rusting brown. The vehicle is a testament to my inability to decide between two good things. A car or a truck, so I compromised with the Ranchero.

Reliable, it fired up immediately, and I headed for home. My bed was calling my name and I wasn't about to ignore it. I was less certain about what I would do in reference to the other 'Calling', whatever it was and whenever it came.

CHAPTER 2

Home for me is a small bungalow in West End, on North Drive, not far from Eastgate Park. Confused? So was I. The real estate sales lady had to drive me there the first time I looked at it.

Not surprisingly, it's located on the west end of St. Louis, about a half hour from my office. The house is small, just two bedrooms, a kitchen, a living room, and a bathroom. I have very little yard and neighbors who are just a little too close. Go figure, a private investigator who likes his privacy.

I pulled into the driveway and parked as an ominous cloud came over the top of the apartment building on the next street. It looks like evening thunderstorms are coming in, and as I walked to the door, the first drops of rain began to fall. Perfect weather for sleeping off the blow to my head, and the pounding that accompanied it.

The small foyer, where I leave my keys on a hook by the door, opens into the living room. Moving through the living room into the kitchen, I found the Tylenol PM in the cabinet over the sink, popped three with a glass of water, and headed for the bedroom.

My bedroom is just that. A room with a bed in it. Room darkening shades and a ceiling fan are the only other things in there. All my clothes hang in the closet, along with my underwear and socks, which are tossed up on the top shelf.

Stripping down to just my underwear, I turned on the fan and climbed into bed. A few minutes later, the pills took effect and I was out cold.

****

"Jack Carter, do you hear me?"

I heard my name and the question, but I didn't know where it came from. I knew I was in bed but that's about all.

"Jack Carter, do you hear me?"

The voice was clear and came with no animosity. In fact, all I could feel was love and peace. I'd never felt so secure in my life, never felt so loved. It could only mean one thing.

"Yes Lord, I hear you."

"Do you love me, Jack Carter?"

"Yes Lord, you know I do."

"You are correct. I wish to call you into my service."

Despite trying to look for a vision or face, there was only the voice. It surrounded me, but felt like it came from inside me.

"I wish to serve but feel incapable. I am a simple man with no special gifts."

It struck me as funny that I was telling the King of Kings who I was. He's omnipotent and omniscient, just your basic all-powerful and all knowing. Seems maybe I was supplying information he already had.

"I will give you all you need and I will always be with you."

"What is it you would have me do, Lord?"

"This call is a life-long mission that will change everything for you. It comes with great sacrifice but great reward as well. I offer you the choice."

"The choice, Lord?"

"This call is as all others, you may choose to follow, or to take your own path. This mission must not be embarked upon without conviction."

Was he kidding? Choose to follow or not! When the Lord makes an offer in person, does anyone say no? Yet I could tell there was no threat in the choice. It's difficult to have private thoughts when you're talking to the 'Lord of Hosts'.

"My call does not come with punishment if you choose another path."

"What is this choice, Lord?"

"My servant will bring the choice before you soon. I have come to signify that the call is real."

The Son of God has come to let you know his offer is for real. I'm no biblical scholar, but I know the Lord's visits with humans have been few and far between. Granted, we interact with him daily through the Holy Spirit, but how many have the Lord show up in their bedroom? And what do you say to him?

"Thank you, Lord."

That's the best I could come up with, and I guess it was enough, because I was quickly back to sleep.

****

The next morning I woke up feeling a little like Ebenezer Scrooge. I've been woke up to pray for people before, especially loved ones who were laid on my heart, but voices from on high were new for me.

I didn't know what to think. Is the Spirit going to be stopping by to talk on a regular basis? Will I ever get a good night's sleep again? More importantly, who's the messenger bringing me the choice I needed to make?

My phone rang. I stared at the caller ID, half-expecting to see Heaven's extension.

Okay, maybe that's a little nuts, but I'm feeling a little odd this morning. It turns out to be my mother.

"Hi, Mom."

"Good Morning, Son. How was your day yesterday?"

"Interesting."

"Oh? How so?"

My mom is Annie Carter, devoted wife of David Carter. She's been alone since we lost Dad to cancer nearly ten years ago, and has made worrying about me her main cause in life.

Mom is my best friend, which tells you something about my social life, but I can talk to her about anything. Almost anything. I'm not ready to try an explanation of 'Big and Black', or the 'Visitor' from last night, even to her.

"Just a lot happening. How are you?"

"I'm good. I wanted to confirm you're coming for dinner tonight."

I'd forgotten, but as of right now, I couldn't think of a reason not to go.

"Yeah, six-thirty okay?"

"Perfect. Why don't you ask that nice cop lady if she wants to come with you? There's plenty of food."

My mom refers to Detective Amanda Myers as 'that cop lady'. She knows her name, but insists on calling her that; I'm not sure why. Mandy Myers is 5' 6" with an athletic build, blonde hair, and green eyes. I'd met her in college, and we've been friends ever since.

Mandy doesn't have a husband, or even a boyfriend yet, which is surprising. She's never met

Mister Right apparently. I fill in on most social engagements, if she needs me to, and I've considered trying to take our friendship to the next level. I never could get up the courage, and I've never revealed how much I adore her.

"Okay, Mom. I'll call her this afternoon and see if she's free."

"Good. I need to pick up a few things still, so I'll see you tonight. Bye."

"Bye."

Hanging up, I listened to my stomach grumble, and thought about eating. Opting to shower first, the hot water brought my body back to life, and washed the blood out of my hair. My head still had a throb to it, but at least it was in the background.

Getting out, I toweled off and donned my normal outfit. Black khaki Dockers, white t-shirt, and black Reebocks. I also have a black bomber jacket I wear when I'm on a case. Mandy says I look like a cross between Fonzie and Johnny Cash. I don't much care, I just know more than once, being all in black has helped me stay hidden when I needed to.

Going into the kitchen, I filled a bowl with Raisin Bran, and sniffed the milk. It seemed reasonably fresh, so I poured it over my cereal, went into the living room, and parked myself in front of the TV. The first spoonful was on its way to my mouth when I heard a knock at the door. Dropping the spoon back in the bowl, I went to answer it.

I opened the door to find Buddy Daniels standing on my step, complete with white robe, leather belt, and large, wooden cross necklace.

I grinned at him. "Yoda!"

Without missing a beat, he looks me up and down, and says, "Fonzie!"

I laughed and invited him in.

"I was just having a bowl of cereal, you hungry?"

"No, but thanks."

I sat down in front of my bowl, and Buddy stood watching me, as I started to eat.

"Buddy, you're making me nervous; grab a seat."

"Thank you."

Buddy pulled the bottom of his robe back and sat in the recliner across from me. Being the sharp private investigator that I am, I suspected his reason for being here was directly tied to my Visitor from last night.

"I suppose there's no point in me asking how you knew where I live."

"It's my mission to know everything I can about you. Please do not be disturbed by it."

"Well Buddy, I hope you'll forgive me, but it does disturb me. I don't know who you are, or why I'm such a fascination to you. Normally, someone who is keeping tabs on a person is up to no good."

He didn't smile, but his eyes remained fixed on me, unflinching. He apparently had nothing to hide. I managed to shovel spoonfuls of cereal into my mouth between questions. The milk on my chin didn't seem to bother him, either.

"It's not my intent to cause you any worry, but my position requires me to do such research."

"Your position?" I asked.

"Yes, I'm a Chaser."

The spoon again stopped halfway to my mouth.

"A what?"

"A Chaser."

"Are you chasing me?"

"No."

"Okay, who are you chasing? Wait, 'Big and Black'?"

"Harbinger is someone that I'm after, but he's not the only one."

"Harbinger? Oh right, Big and Black."

"Yes."

"Strange name. What is a Chaser, anyway?"

Up until now, Buddy had sat motionless in the recliner, watching me eat. With my last question, he sat forward, and lowered his voice.

"Did you have a Visitor last night?"

"I'm betting you know I did."

"The Visitor told you of a choice, correct?"

"Same statement as the last one, you know He did."

"I am here to present you with that choice."

Fortunately, I had finished my cereal, because suddenly I wasn't hungry.

"You're the servant I was told about?"

"I am."

CHAPTER 3

Twenty-four hours ago, I was an ordinary guy. Just an ordinary guy, with an ordinary life, he tried to live the best he could. A Christian who loved his God, and tried to demonstrate it in the way he conducted himself. No one special, or so I thought.

I'd been taught God has a purpose for everyone's life, and I assumed mine was to pray for others, maybe volunteer at church, or something similar. I'd never been a hundred percent sure what my particular mission was, but be a Chaser?

Buddy sat watching me for a reaction. So far, he'd been disappointed.

"Okay Buddy, run this at me one more time. What is a Chaser?"

He began the explanation for the third time, with no apparent impatience.

"When a person dies, they cross over to the other side, and into the presence of God. It's the time when the 'white light' stories you hear, happen. During this time of crossing over, there are some individuals with the ability to resist the light. They don't want to complete the journey, for one reason or another, and decide to run."

I held up my hand.

"Run? What do you mean by run?"

"They're referred to as 'Runners', but what they've done is tried to return to earth. They seek to resume their life, despite the fact that they are dead, and attempt to circumvent God's plan."

"No coming back from the dead for us?"

"Exactly, it is not for us to decide if the time of our death is convenient or not."

"And you chase them?"

"Yes."

"And return them to the 'white light' path?"

"Correct."

"And the choice I have is to accept the mission of a Chaser or not?"

"Yes."

I stood up and carried my bowl to the sink. Buddy's eyes followed me, but he didn't say anything.

When I returned to the room, I started to laugh; I couldn't help myself.

Buddy didn't see the humor.

"What are you laughing about?"

"What am I laughing about? Take your pick! The concept of Runners and Chasers, or that someone would try to outrun God, or that you're sitting here asking me to fulfill my calling as a Chaser, or maybe just the craziness of the last twenty-four hours. It's all so incredible as to be ridiculous!"

"Do not mock the call of God." He said it quietly, strongly, but without any malice.

"I'm not, at least, I don't mean to. There's so many questions to ask, ramifications to consider, and I don't know where to start. For instance, what's the job pay?"

I told you I'm sarcastic when I'm scared.

"There is no *pay* for this ministry!"

"I'm just kidding, Buddy."

I returned to my seat, and looked him directly in the eyes. What I really needed to know had nothing to do with how it all worked, or what the day-to-day life of a Chaser was like. What really mattered was inside Buddy.

"How long?"

He looked confused.

"How long what?"

"How long have you been doing this? How long is the call for?"

His face softened, and his voice became strong, filled with pride.

"Thirty-five years, I've served for thirty-five years," He paused before finishing. "The choice to serve is for life."

I could see it in him, but I needed to hear it.

"Are you at peace with the choice you made?"

For the first time since he came through the door, Buddy Daniels smiled. Not just a little grin, but a wide smile of joy.

"I am."

****

I arrived downtown about an hour after Buddy had left. He told me to pray about things and seek guidance from the Spirit. I wanted to ask a thousand questions.

"In time," he'd said while he patted my shoulder. "The decision is not to be made rashly, so we'll talk soon."

"What if I decided it's not for me, and said no? Do you have some sort of mind erasing trick to do on me?"

He'd laughed.

"You mean like 'Men in Black', flash a ray in your eyes, and it's all gone?"

Okay, I agree. It sounded a little crazy, but at this point, all bets were off.

"Yeah, something like that. You know, keep me from telling anyone about you."

A grin curled across his lips.

"Do you really want to tell people you were asked to be a Spirit Chaser by an old man in a white robe?"

It'd been my turn to laugh.

"Point taken!"

I parked the Ranchero on the street and made my way to the top of the stairs. This time without being hit on the head, and let myself into the office. A pile of mail lay on the floor where it had fallen through the slot in the door. I gathered it up, scanned it quickly, deciding it to be the usual junk. I punched the button on the answering machine.

"You have three new messages. Message one- 'Mr. Carter, this is Libby Samms. I need an update on my husband's case. Please call me as soon as possible'."

I made a note to call her. She thought her husband was cheating on her, but I'd found he was working a second job in order to pay for a surprise anniversary trip. Now I needed to find a way to tell her he wasn't cheating without spoiling it.

"Message two- 'Mr. Carter, This is James Dobbs. Please call my office to discuss terms of a contract for your services. ICM has an issue we need to investigate per our last conversation'."

He left his number, which I already had, and hung up. Intercontinental Machines had someone they suspected of disability insurance fraud, and I'd worked cases for them before.

"Message three- 'Hi, Jack. It's me. Just calling to see what's up. Give me a ring'."

The last message was Mandy. I picked up the phone and dialed her personal number.

"Hello."

"Hey, Mandy."

"Hi Jack, How's it going?"

I wanted to tell her everything, to get her take on the choice, and see what she would do. I knew I couldn't.

"Same old thing, you?"

"I managed to wreck another car."

We laughed. Mandy had a reputation for putting police department cars out of commission. Usually, she was taking a fugitive down with the front bumper, or some other such thing. She also managed to make some of the cars fail mechanically, with an almost eerie regularity. No car assigned to her had lasted more than a year. Good thing she's an excellent detective.

"What happened this time?"

"A guy tried to take off in his car as we went to serve him an arrest warrant. My car happened to get parked in his way."

"Funny how it's always your car in the way."

"I know; weird right?"

I remembered my mom's dinner.

"What are you doin' tonight?"

"Well, I had a date, but he cancelled. Why?"

"His loss. Mom's cooking me dinner, and she said there's lots. Want to come?"

"Sure, did she call me 'that cop lady' again?"

I laughed.

Despite knowing Mandy since college, she'd only recently met my mother. Mandy had joined the force in Kansas City after graduation, and hadn't met my mom until she moved to St. Louis a year ago. We'd maintained our friendship by making the drive on I-70 across the state occasionally, to go to a ball game, or do some fishing. A detective job in St. Louis brought her here.

"Yes, I think she likes you."

"The feeling is mutual. Pick you up at home?"

"Sure, sixish?"

"See you then."

After we hung up, I found myself unable to sit still. I paced the office, trying to sort out my thoughts. One thing had my attention now, and it wasn't an investigation, but a decision.

CHAPTER 4

At six sharp, Mandy rolled up in her bright, yellow VW bug. The car is a stark contrast to the black sedan she drives all day on the job. The sunroof open, she stayed in the car as I locked up, and I was taken aback when I got into the car.

Instead of the usual jeans and a sweatshirt, she's wearing beige khakis and an orange sleeveless blouse. She had her hair pulled up in a bun, and she wore sandals, instead of sneakers.

"Wow, don't you look nice!"

"Thank you, sir. I decided tonight is the night I do away with the "cop lady" name from your mom."

"Well, this should do it."

She pulled away from the curb as we began the fifteen-minute drive to Mom's house. I remembered our conversation from earlier.

"Sooo, what's the verdict on your department car?"

"Jerry told me it would live to fight another day. I'm using a black and white until it's done."

"Must be weird being a detective and pulling up in a patrol car?"

"Yeah, I get a few grins from the other detectives, but they also know I'm the one who nailed the creep."

We were on Kings Highway, and the wind through the sunroof made talking difficult. I reached up and slid the roof most of the way closed. Mandy gave me a funny look.

"Speaking of weird, I have something I've been thinking about, and I'd like your take on it."

"Okay, shoot."

"We both believe we're going to heaven when we die, right?" She nodded and I continued. "But have you ever thought about what the few moments after death will contain?"

She glanced at me with a grin.

"That's out of blue, what's up?"

"Just something I've been thinking about."

She got a serious look on her face as she considered her answer.

"Yeah, I've thought about it. Mostly, when I see one of those shows with people describing the white light, and the peace they feel. I guess that matches what I hope will happen."

"I guess the white light makes sense, we know God is light."

She snorted.

"Sure, but some people go to hell. I wouldn't think white light would be down *that* path."

I thought about that for a minute as Mandy took us off the loop onto Natural Bridge Avenue.

"Well, we know we're all going to stand before God to be judged, so maybe the dark light comes after that."

"Makes sense I guess."

Mandy turned down Marcus Avenue, my mom's street, and slowed the car to a stop in front of the house. She turned the car off, and looked sideways at me. I had one more question.

"What if during that few moments when you crossover, you decide you don't want to go yet? You think we can change our path, make a run for it?"

I could see Detective Myers take over inside her.

"What's this all about?"

Time to change the subject. Detective Myers was too smart for me to tangle with, and I'd already decided she wasn't getting the full story, at least not yet.

"No big deal, just some weird thoughts I've been having."

Her green eyes focused in on me, and I suddenly felt like a suspect.

"You gonna' die on me or something?"

That caught me off guard and I started to laugh.

"No, no. Nothing like that."

From the corner of my eye, I saw Mom at the door. Exit stage left.

"Come on, let's go. Mom's at the door."

Mandy looked up, and broke into a smile, seemingly distracted. I knew it was only temporary.

We got out and walked up to the door where Mom waited, clearly impressed with Mandy's outfit.

"Mandy, you look adorable!"

Mandy gave me a quick 'I told you so look' as we went through the front door. No more cop lady.

****

Dinner consisted of one of my favorites, Mom's lasagna, along with salad. For dessert, homemade cheesecake. It's a wonder I ever left home.

After dinner, we were sitting in the living room having coffee when Mandy proved she'd only been temporarily distracted from our conversation in the car.

"Mrs. Carter…"

"Annie, please. You make me feel so old calling me Mrs. Carter."

"Sorry… Annie, Jack asked me a very interesting question on the way over here."

Oh, no. She wasn't gonna' do what I think she's gonna' do, is she?

"Really? What was that?"

They were both looking at me now.

"He asked me if I thought people could change their path after they die."

Mom eyed me suspiciously.

"Change their path how, Jack?"

Oh, crap. She did do what I thought she was gonna' do.

"I don't know, like when you're crossing over to the other side, what if you're not ready to go?"

His mother smiled.

"Jack, you know the bible says nothing about us having control over such things."

"Yeah, I know. I was just thinking about the white light and all that stuff."

My mom chuckled, but Mandy was studying me with a serious expression. I needed a distraction and fast.

"Mandy, did you tell Mom about the latest mishap with your department car?"

Mandy glared at me, but proceeded to tell the story, as I got myself another cup of coffee. I should've kept my mouth shut on the way over here, but too late; I'll have to avoid any more questions on the way home.

****

It turned out I didn't have to stonewall Mandy on the way home. She'd let the questions drop in favor of going on about the dinner.

"You're so lucky. My mom, *when* she cooked, specialized in macaroni and cheese. That lasagna was unbelievable! I love going over there, so ask me anytime."

The way Mandy looked tonight, I might be asking her to have dinner at my mom's house every other day. Of course, I've seen her dressed up before, but I never tire of it.

"I'm certainly blessed to be her son, and I'm glad you had a good time."

She parked in front of my house and I got out. I came around and stood next to her car window.

"Talk to you tomorrow?"

She put the car in reverse and started to back up.

"Probably. Goodnight."

I waved and turned towards the door. As I put the key in the lock, I heard a noise to my right. Out of the shadows stepped Harbinger, his gray eyes glowing in the darkness. I stepped away from the door but didn't run. I recoiled a little at the guttural noise of his voice as he stepped closer.

"Did you receive your calling?"

"What, no blow to the back of the head this time?"

He took another step closer.

"Did you receive your calling?"

"You seemed to know more about this than I do, why don't you tell me?"

Despite my obvious insolence, he seemed unfazed.

"I know the Chaser who seeks to mentor you. I am going to destroy him, and if your follow his lead, I will destroy you as well."

"The way I understand it, you've been trying to 'destroy' him for nearly thirty years. If you're so sure you can kill him, what's taking so long?"

His eyes flared even brighter, and a growl rose from somewhere deep inside him.

"If you join with the Chaser, I will come for you."

Something about these two encounters was gnawing at me, and suddenly, I knew what it was.

"Why are you warning me and, if you're so determined to kill me, why wait? You had me tied to a chair and left me alive."

The eyes watched me for several moments before, without warning, he disappeared. His vanishing act seems to be the only thing he *doesn't* warn me about.

I stood outside, making sure he'd left for good, before looking around my neighborhood.

Did anyone see me talking to Harbinger? Was he invisible to others? Did I look like I was talking to a bush?

Time to get inside.

I let myself in and locked the door behind me. Dinner had made me sleepy, but Harbinger had ruined my plans for going to bed.

I couldn't figure why he was so intent on warning me about following Buddy.

What is his stake in keeping me from answering the call on my life? What was he afraid of?

The obvious finally occurred to me.

He's a Runner! But why is he so concerned about me if Buddy hadn't been able to catch him in the last thirty years? Harbinger fears me answering the call. No, can't be.

I needed Buddy Daniels to answer some of these questions before I could make the decision to follow, but inside I felt my spirit crying out, '*go for it!*'

Harbinger is big and scary, but for some reason, I wasn't afraid tonight.

I needed to talk to Buddy and I wanted it to be tonight. I grabbed my car keys and headed for the door.

Wait! I don't know where Buddy lives. I can't go there if I want to. Crap!

I hung the keys back up and went to bed. Eventually, I fell asleep.

CHAPTER 5

The next morning I was up early.

I'm a private investigator; I can find Mr. Buddy Daniels.

My plan was to go to the office and do my normal process of ferreting out a person whose only information I had was their name. Usually, I can scare up an address, and find somebody within a few hours, but I outdid myself this morning.

He was waiting for me in my car.

I guess he figured it was no use hiding from a sharp P.I. like me. I got in my Ranchero, which I was pretty sure had been locked last night. He spoke without looking at me.

"Good morning."

"Good morning to you. How long you been out here?"

"Not long. I have something to do, and I wanted you to come along."

"Are we going chasing?"

A smile crossed his face.

"How did you know?"

I tapped my temple.

"Private investigator, remember?"

I started the car and backed out onto the street.

"Which way?"

"Take Kings Highway north to Florissant, then east to Gano."

"Okay, you're the navigator."

Despite all the questions I had from the night before, I sensed Buddy wanted to focus. He didn't speak, so I didn't pry.

When we got to Gano Street in the north end of the city, he told me to park across from a sprawling, red brick building. Bryan Elementary is the classic, inner-city school building. Resembling a brick castle, with ivy growing on it, and white cement windowsills. It's in better condition than most schools the same age.

I could see the playground from where we sat, asphalt-covered, surrounded with black rod-iron fence. The area had recently been stocked with new plastic swings, slides, and ladders. Kids played in the July sun, and I could only assume it was summer school.

"Give me your hand?"

It was Buddy, and he was staring into my eyes.

"What?"

"Give me your hand."

I did. He held it with his right and put his left hand over my eyes.

"Dear Lord, I seek the power of sight for Jack. Let him see the things he must see this day, and may your understanding be in him. In Jesus name, amen."

I repeated 'Amen' , blinked, and stared at Buddy. I didn't feel any different. Buddy got out of the car, and looked back through the window.

"Coming?"

Heck yeah, I'm coming!

"Right behind you."

Buddy was leaning against the fence, watching the kids play, when I caught up with him. No one seemed to notice us, and after a few minutes, Buddy looked at me.

"You see her?"

"See who?"

"The mother, she's over there."

I followed his gaze towards the far side of the playground. Standing by the entrance to the playground was a woman. She was thin and tall, with brown hair hanging loosely to her shoulders. Despite the July heat, she wore a beige, long-sleeve sweater.

"Her?"

"Yes her."

"You called her the mother; whose mother?"

"The little girl over there is her daughter."

Alone on a ledge, not far from the door into the school, sat a young girl who wasn't playing with the other kids. Thin with brown hair, her resemblance to the mother was obvious.

Buddy started to walk the sidewalk around the fence towards where the mother stood.

"Come on."

As we came around the corner and approached, she didn't seem to notice our presence. Buddy stopped and whispered.

"You stay here. Watch carefully."

Buddy, wearing his robe, moved up next to the woman. She turned and surprise was evident on her face. Buddy began to speak to her, but I couldn't make out what he was saying.

The woman nodded several times before looking towards the playground. When she looked back at Buddy, tears were rolling down her cheeks. Buddy spoke to her again, and she nodded once more. Again, she looked towards the little girl sitting alone.

Finally, without taking her eyes off the little girl, she reached out towards Buddy. She took hold of the oversize wooden cross around his neck, a flash of light blinded me, and the woman was gone.

Buddy came walking back towards me, a smile on his face. I was stunned.

"What happened? Where'd she go?"

Buddy passed me, walking towards the car.

"She's crossed over."

I was struggling to keep up, both physically and mentally.

"Was she a runner?"

"Yes."

"Why did she run?"

"She was an atheist. When she began to crossover, she realized God is real, and wanted to warn her daughter."

We reached the car, and stood on opposite sides, facing each other over the hood.

"Did you kill her?"

"No, I didn't need to."

"Why not?"

"She went voluntarily."

We got in the Ranchero and I started to drive. I tried to sort out my thoughts for a few minutes before starting the questions again.

"How was she going to warn her daughter, wasn't she a spirit?"

"Indeed, she was. Runners get stronger with every passing day. They eventually get the power to become corporeal."

"You mean human again?"

"Not exactly. They can manifest to be seen, touch things, write things, and so on."

We'd only gone a short distance when we came to O'Fallon City Park. I pulled into the parking lot and stopped the car. I can talk and drive, but this was too much to take in.

"So eventually she would've become strong enough, to contact her daughter, and tell her about God?"

"Yes."

"Wait a second! Doesn't God want all people to believe in him? Why wouldn't he want the girl to be told about Him?"

Buddy sighed.

"That was my exact thought when I saw my mentor, Justin, crossover someone for the first time. But the dynamic changes after you're dead. While we live on this earth, we have the choice of salvation through Christ, or not. But when we die, the choice dies with us. Anyone who tries to change the way God set it up, is trying to circumvent God's plan."

"So what if the mother had been successful?"

"You mean if she'd warned her daughter?"

"Yeah, then what?"

"The Holy Spirit would take her."

"Take her? What does that mean?"

"She would've died."

"The little girl?"

"Yes."

I was stunned, again.

How could the Holy Spirit kill someone?

Buddy sat looking straight ahead, not moving, waiting for my next question.

"Why?"

"God seeks a people who worship by freewill. The mother warning the girl would remove the daughter's freewill choice. Therefore, she must be taken in her current state of salvation, whatever it is."

I sat for a minute and tried to let sink in what Buddy was saying. Eventually, I started the car, and headed for home. We didn't speak the rest of the way, and when we arrived, he got out. Shutting the door, he looked back at me through the window.

"Have you figured it out yet?"

I had.

"You told the mother if she warned her child, the child would die, and her chance to be saved lost. She chose to crossover, and give her daughter the chance to live her life, to find God on her own."

"Exactly. We spared her daughter's life by making her mother crossover."

"How did you do it? I mean I saw the flash of light, but how?"

"This cross," he lifted the oversize cross on his chest. "Is made from the Cedars of Lebanon. It's blessed and imbued with the power of the Chaser. When she took hold, it sent her over."

My mind spun. Information overload had taken hold, and I needed a break. My office and some mundane sleuthing seemed to be in order.

"I'll talk to you later, Buddy."

He turned and walked towards his car.

"Sounds good."

****

An hour later, I had let myself into my office, and listened to my messages.

I made an appointment for this afternoon to meet Mrs. Samms at the Heritage Cafeteria. I still hadn't figured out how I was going to tell her about her husband's second job, without spoiling the surprise, but I figured I could come up with something at the last minute.

I decided to bounce another question off Mandy, and hope she wouldn't react like the other night. I'd felt like a cornered rat when she started grilling me. I dialed her number.

"Hello."

"Hey Mandy, it's me. You busy?"

"Not at the moment, what's up?"

"I wanting your take on something else I've been thinking of."

"Shoot."

Suddenly, I wasn't sure how to word it. In fact, I wasn't sure what it was I wanted to ask her. I guess I just wanted to talk to someone that wasn't a spirit, or chasing a spirit. She sensed my hesitation.

"Jack? What is it?"

"Nothing, I'm sorry to bug you."

"You know you can call me anytime, to talk about anything, right?"

"I know, and thanks."

I could tell she was waiting for me to tell her why I called, but I changed the subject instead.

"You had a good time last night?"

"You know I did. Is there something else?"

"No. I gotta meet a client, so I'll talk to you later."

"Okaaaay. Nice not talking to you, Jack."

"Same here."

I hung up feeling more than a little foolish. I checked my watch, and realized I needed to hurry, if I was going to be on time to meet Mrs. Samms.

****

Heritage Cafeteria is only four blocks from my office and a walk, even though it was quite warm out, seemed inviting. Even if it made me a little late, maybe I could come up with what I was going to say to Mrs. Samms, before I got there.

A few minutes later, I arrived to find Mrs. Samms sitting near the front window with a cup of coffee. I got myself one and joined her.

"Hello, Mr. Carter. You have news about my husband?"

An attractive lady, with jet-black hair and a pale complexion, she had bright blue eyes, and a smile that normally revealed a set of perfect white teeth. She wasn't smiling at the moment, and appeared quite tense, as I sat across from her at the table.

"Yes, ma'am. I've finished with your case."

"Really? And what did you find? Is my husband cheating on me?"

"No, Mrs. Samms. I couldn't find any evidence of another woman in his life."

She looked skeptical, as if I was holding something back. Of course I was, but not what she thought.

"Well, where is he going after work three times a week? He keeps telling me not to worry, it's nothing."

I pulled out my bill, put it under a picture, and slid both across the table in her direction. The picture showed her husband entering a downtown bar. He worked three nights a week as a bartender there. She looked at it, then me.

"A bar? He's going to a bar, but no woman is meeting him?"

"That's correct. On three separate occasions, I followed him in, and observed what he was doing. He was at the bar, talked to anyone who talked to him, and watched some sports."

'A half-truth is a whole lie', but I was sure she would understand when she got the rest of the story from her husband. Everything I had seen indicated Mr. Samms loved his wife, and was faithful.

"He can watch sports at home. It doesn't make any sense."

"Sometimes men need guy time."

"I guess."

She looked at my bill before pulling her checkbook out of her purse. She wrote the check and handed it to me.

"Thank you, Mr. Carter."

"You're welcome, Mrs. Samms."

I watched her walk away, and was about to leave myself, when I noticed a man standing near the door. Tall and thin, with black hair, he appeared to be in his early forties. He didn't have any food or drink; nor was he in line to order.

A teenage girl, wearing black khaki's and a white button-down shirt, moved food trays between the kitchen and the serving tables. She was bringing hot food out to the cafeteria line, and returning empty pans to the kitchen. Despite his obvious staring, the dark-haired girl didn't seem to notice the man.

People walked in front of the man, without excusing themselves, and he didn't speak to them. He would rush forward, say something to the girl, but she refused to look at him. In fact, she acted as if he wasn't there.

My curiosity got the better of me. I left my table, walking towards him, and he seemed to notice me immediately. When I reached him, I started to ask what he was doing. Fear crossed his face and he bolted for the door.

I followed him out of the restaurant, several steps behind. When I got outside, he was nowhere in sight.

Weird. But then again, my life seemed to functioning on the 'weird' setting these days.

I turned and started walking back towards my office when I spotted a white robe headed my direction. I stopped and waited until Buddy got to me.

I laughed.

"I guess I shouldn't be surprised to see you here, but let me say it anyway. What are you doing here?"

I noticed, despite wearing a robe in July, he didn't appear to be sweating. He took me by the elbow, and steered me towards a bench not far from where we stood.

"I've been following someone, and they happened to cross paths with you, it wasn't intentional."

"Do you mean chasing someone?"

"Yes."

Two and two finally started to add up to four in my head.

"This guy you were chasing…"

"I didn't say it was a man."

"Okay, but if I'm right, he was tall, thin with black hair."

"Yes."

"I saw him in the cafeteria. He freaked when he saw me."

Buddy gave me that 'figure it out for yourself' look. I ran the events in the restaurant back through my head, then snapped my fingers.

"It wasn't that he saw me, it was that I saw him, right?"

Buddy looked pleased.

"Correct. He knew if you could see him, you might be able to send him back. That's why he ran."

"But why could I see him?"

"The prayer from the school opened your eyes, and they will stay open as long as you stay on the path. If you choose not to chase, the sight will be removed."

Made sense to me, I guess.

"Who's the girl?"

"The one he was watching?"

I nodded.

"A daughter he never knew in life. He wanted to meet her before he crossed over, and he didn't believe me when I told him he would end her life by contacting her."

"Did you get him to crossover?"

He nodded.

"How? I mean, I know how it happens when they agree, but what about someone like him?"

He pulled back the hem of his robe to reveal the short wooden sword.

"You stabbed him with that? Kinda dull, isn't it?"

"He was spirit when I pierced him. Neither the cross nor the sword will work if they are manifested in human form."

My head was beginning to spin again, and the time seemed right for more coffee, espresso this time.

"I'm running over to Starbucks, you want something?"

He shook his head, reached in to his pocket, and pulled out a piece of paper. He handed it to me, and I read the address.

"What's this?"

"My address. Can you come for lunch tomorrow? I want you to meet my Sarah."

"Your Sarah? You're married?"

"Yes, why so surprised?"

I thought about it. Yoda wasn't married, or was he?

"I guess I thought chasing precluded any personal life."

He smiled.

"I wouldn't have made it this long in my ministry without her support."

I looked at the address. It was on the outskirts of the city on the south side.

"What time should I be there?"

"One okay?"

"I'll see you then. Should I bring anything?"

"No, and come alone. We'll be talking about things that must remain between us."

I got up and headed for the Starbucks.

"Okay, one it is. Bye."

CHAPTER 6

I left home around noon for my lunch date at Buddy and Sarah Daniels home. Taking Interstate 55 south out of St. Louis, I rode for nearly twenty minutes before exiting. Two right turns and I was on Primm Street, which the Daniels lived on.

It should not have come as a surprise their house backed up on a cemetery, but sure enough, it did. Saints Peter and Paul Cemetery, one of the biggest in the area. I wondered if being a Chaser meant I'd have to move next to a cemetery.

I found the house at the end of the block and parked by the curb.

Buddy and Sarah lived in a small matchbox house, yellow with a white shingle roof, and white trim. Two windows ran across the front of the house, one on either side of the front door, and each was shaded by a white aluminum awning.

The lawn was green and manicured, divided in two sections by a cement walk leading up from the street to the house. The only tree, a towering oak in the backyard, shaded most of the small house from the mid-day sun.

Getting out, I reached into the passenger seat to retrieve the flowers I'd brought with me. Mandy had insisted a good guest would not come empty handed the first time he visited someone's home. I talked to her last night and she was quick to make sure I was up on my etiquette.

As I reached to push the bell, the door came open, and Buddy was standing there. No robe, no cross, and no sword. Just bright red, Bermuda shorts and a yellow t-shirt.

"Hi, Jack. Come on in."

He swung the screen door open and I stepped in. I could hear Mrs. Daniels calling from the kitchen.

"Is that Jack?"

Buddy gestured to the kitchen, ahead on the right, and I followed him.

The kitchen was done in the same bright colors as the outside of the house, with white appliances, white countertop, and cabinet's painted pale yellow. This might be the cheeriest house I'd ever been in. I think the kitchen curtains had yellow smiley faces, but they were pulled back, so I couldn't be sure.

Sarah Daniels turned and walked towards me. A tiny woman with white hair, her smile took up half her face. She wore an orange sundress with a white belt. With a delicate nose and bright eyes, she radiated joy. Both of the Daniels were barefoot.

"Jack, it's so nice to meet you. I've heard a lot about you from Buddy."

She wiped her palms on her apron and shook my hand. She had the grip of an ironworker.

"Thank you, Mrs. Daniels."

"Oh, no you don't. Sarah will be just fine. We're not nearly so formal around here."

"Sarah it is. These are for you."

She took the flowers I held out to her, and her smile grew even larger, which I thought was impossible. I loved this woman and I'd just met her.

"They're beautiful! Thank you so much."

As she went to put them in water, Buddy led me into the backyard. A small patio formed from randomly placed cement stones held a table and four chairs. A pitcher of something cold sat on the table.

"Ice tea, Jack?"

"Yes, thanks."

He poured me a glass and stepped over to the barbeque to check on lunch. I stared over the back fence at the huge cemetery, row after row of stones, among manicured greenery. I realized it was quite peaceful.

"Some view you have here, Buddy."

He glanced over his shoulder as he flipped some steaks.

"Yeah. Some people would be creeped out by a cemetery, but we find it quiet and serene."

"Must make it handy when you're chasing."

Buddy laughed.

"You'd think so, but not really. Most Runners are trying to get somewhere other than a cemetery, and I almost never find them there."

I wore gray shorts and a blue St. Louis Rams t-shirt. I also had on sandals, but I slipped them off to stand in the cool grass.

"How long have you lived here?"

"Twenty-eight years. We bought the house when we got married, and never felt the need to move."

I did some quick math in my head.

"So you married Sarah *after* you became a Chaser?"

The door opened and Sarah came out carrying a plate of cut-up watermelon.

"That's right. He told me before we were married, but I didn't see how it made any difference. We all need to serve God in whatever fashion the Lord asks, and Buddy had found his calling. What more could a

Christian woman ask for than a man whose priority was his wife and his God."

I took a piece of the watermelon and sat in a chair.

"What about the danger?"

She shrugged her shoulders.

"God called him, so I let God take care of him."

"Don't you worry?"

"Sure I worry, I'm human, but I take comfort in prayer. Buddy has told me he can feel my prayers when he's in a tight spot."

Buddy was taking the steaks off the grill and nodding his head at the same time.

"Prayer is powerful. In fact, it's the Christians most powerful weapon against evil. Steaks are ready, let's eat!"

****

Lunch consisted of the steaks, homemade mashed potatoes, garden salad, and fresh-baked chocolate chip cookies for dessert.

I groaned as I took my third cookie.

"That was fantastic! My microwave dinners just don't measure up."

Sarah was gathering the plates.

"I'm very pleased you liked it. I have dishes and a kitchen to clean up, so I'll leave you two alone for awhile."

I started to get up.

"Let me help."

Sarah wagged her finger at me.

"You're our guest. I appreciate the offer, but I'll handle it."

There was no room for argument and I retook my seat. She was gone, with her arms loaded, in less than a minute.

"You're a blessed man, Buddy Daniels. If she was twenty years younger, I'd steal her from you."

He looked at the door and back at me, a smile lighting his face.

"Yes, yes I am. You want more tea?"

I shook my head, and his smile vanished, as his demeanor turned serious. He regarded me as if sizing me up.

"How's it going?"

"You mean with the decision process?"

He nodded.

"I don't know how I feel. I'm in awe of what you do, and don't know if I'm capable of the same."

"God not only calls us, but He equips us."

"I know, I know. One thing I was wondering about, do you have like a territory? I mean, how far do you go when you chase? I'm sure Runners aren't limited to St. Louis."

Buddy allowed himself to laugh before answering.

"No, I'm not the only one, and St. Louis isn't the only city with runners. There are many others called to chase, but we have very limited contact with each other."

"Why? I would think you would want to support each other, or even pray together."

"Like everything, God has a plan, and a regular meeting between Chasers is not part of the plan. It's not that I avoid other Chasers, but more that God keeps me focused on what I must do, not what he is doing elsewhere."

"Have you ever worked together with other Chasers on a case?"

"No," his face clouded over and his eyes turned sad. "The only Chaser I've ever worked with was my mentor, and it didn't turn out well."

"What happened?"

Buddy hesitated.

"Justin was killed during a chase we were on."

I wanted to ask more, and understand the events leading up to the death of a chaser, but Buddy was not in the mood.

"I don't want to discuss that tonight, maybe another time, but tonight is about you," He sipped his ice tea. "I have a runner I'm working on, who I think I can surprise tomorrow. Want to go?"

"Sure, I'm in. Where and when?"

"I'll call you in the morning with the details. I've still got a little research to do."

"The research and how you find these Runners is something I need to know more about."

Again, he laughed.

"You're a P.I. aren't you? You think that's by accident?"

I hadn't thought of it that way. God had guided me to this profession as a means of preparation.

"How do you get the information on who you're chasing?"

"That is best learned by experience."

Oh, great. Suddenly he's going all 'mystery answers' on me again.

I looked around and realized it was dark. A quick glance at my watch surprised me. Ten-thirty.

"I guess I'd better go. This was a wonderful evening, Buddy. Thanks."

He got up and I followed him into the house. Sarah was putting the last dish in the strainer, and turned to say goodbye.

"Nice to meet you, Jack."

"Nice to meet you, Sarah. Thanks again for the meal."

"Anytime."

Buddy walked me to the front door. I turned to him once outside.

“See you tomorrow?”

“Yup. I’ll call with the time and place. Goodnight.”

He closed the door and I went to the Ranchero. I couldn’t decide which was more full, my stomach or my head. Whichever, both were feeling very satisfied tonight.

CHAPTER 7

The next morning, and I use the term 'morning' loosely, the vibrating of my cell phone next to my bed, roused me from a deep sleep. I picked it up and looked at the time before answering. Five a.m.

"Hello?"

"Time to go, Jack. I'll bethere in half an hour."

"I thought you said 'tomorrow morning' you would call?"

"It's past midnight, that's morning. See you in thirty minutes."

He hung up before I could protest any further. Dragging myself out of bed, I showered, and put on my regular working clothes, this time including the black, bomber jacket.

A bowl of cereal and half a cup of coffee later, the sun began to peak over the horizon, followed closely by Buddy pulling up in the driveway. I went out to his car and got in.

"You always up this early?"

He shook his head.

"Nope. In fact, some nights I don't go to bed. Last night was one of those nights."

I glanced over at him and could see no perceptible signs of him being sleep-deprived. To me, he looked the fresher of the two of us.

"What did you do all night?"

"I told you, research."

"All night?"

"No, I spent several hours in prayer. You will as well, if you choose to become a Chaser. You must be as ready spiritually, as you are mentally and physically, when you go after a runner."

"Makes sense."

Buddy's car is a white, late model Chevy Impala. Comfortable and ordinary, not one that would attract attention. He backed out the driveway and headed east.

I've never been what you would call a 'prayer warrior', and the thought of hours of prayer seemed impossible to me.

"Don't get me wrong, but how do you pray for such a long time?"

He chuckled.

"I asked my mentor the same question."

"And what did he say?"

"He told me I wouldn't notice the time because I was talking with the Spirit. He said I would come to treasure prayer time," He glanced over at me. "He was right."

I looked up and noticed we were coming into the downtown area of the city. Getting off the Interstate loop, we drove down near the Arch, and parked behind the Drury Hotel. The sun was fully up, but downtown was still quiet. Just a few cars coming and going in front of the hotel. The usual parade of tourists, filing from various parking spots in the area towards the Arch, had not yet begun.

Buddy hadn't said anything since we parked, but I noticed he was staring directly at the hotel dumpster. I followed his gaze and spotted a man standing behind the trash container, watching the back door of the hotel.

"Is that him?"

Buddy nodded. "His name is Stan Warren."

The man looked to be a little under six foot tall, balding, but muscular. He wore jeans and a t-shirt, and didn't appear to notice us. Buddy got out of the car, shut the door, and stuck his head back in the window.

"Follow, slightly off to the side, twenty feet behind me."

I got out and kept my distance as Buddy approached the man. Buddy had his robe on along with the cross. I assumed the sword was in his belt. The man didn't see Buddy until they were just a few feet apart.

"Stan Warren?"

Stan's head swiveled to look at the Chaser, and anger crossed his face.

"Who are you?"

"That's not important. I'm here because it's time for you to go."

"I don't know you, or why you can see me, but I'm not going anywhere."

"Oh, come now. Let's not be difficult."

Buddy's voice was calm, but I sensed a tightness in his stance. Like a coiled snake, he watched Stan warily. The runner tried to ignore Buddy, turning constantly to look at the back door of the hotel. Buddy stepped closer.

"I can't let you follow through with your plan."

Stan turned to face the Chaser.

"Oh yeah, and what's that?"

"You can't get revenge from beyond the grave. Vengeance belongs to the Lord."

Stan Warren's image suddenly transformed, taking on solid shape, which was absent before. He swung out and struck Buddy flush on the side of his head, knocking him to the ground. Before I could even react, Buddy was back up.

Sweeping his leg under the Runner, he took his feet out from under the man. When Stan hit the ground, he returned to spirit, and Buddy pounced. With practiced efficiency, Buddy drew the sword, and plunged it into the man's chest. A brilliant flash and Stan Warren was gone.

Buddy straightened up and put away his sword. A welt was coming up on the side of his face, but he didn't seem to notice. My heart was pounding, and I was having a hard time grasping how quick everything had happened. Buddy looked at me.

"You okay?"

"Me?" I was incredulous. "I'm fine. You're the one who has the welt on his face, are you okay?"

He reached up and touched his face.

"Oh yeah, minor bump. Let's get back in the car."

I followed him back to the Impala and we got in. He pointed.

"Watch the hotel back door."

A few minutes later, another man about the same age as Stan Warren, came out wearing the uniform of the Drury Hotel. Buddy could apparently see my confusion and explained.

"That's Jeff Deaver. He was best man at Stan Warren's wedding to Judy. Twelve years later, Jeff and Judy are having an affair. Stan found out, and was on his way to confront his friend, when he was killed in a car wreck."

I watched Jeff Deaver get into his car and drive away.

"Stan was here to kill his former friend?"

"Yes. I'd been chasing Stan for several weeks, trying to get a handle on why he was running. It wasn't until after I discovered the affair, and where Jeff Deaver worked, I was able to find the spot to confront Stan Warren."

Buddy started the car as I tried to organize my thoughts.

"What happened right before he struck you? He changed somehow."

"He went corporeal."

"Corporeal? You mean physical?"

"Sort of. In order to kill Jeff, or attack me, he had to manifest."

It was beginning to sink in how this job could be dangerous.

"You knocked him down before attacking him? Why not just run him through with the sword?"

"Remember, the wooden sword is dull, it's a spiritual weapon."

The light bulb went on.

"So he had to be spirit when you stabbed him."

"Exactly, and knocking him down caused him to lose both the focus and the energy necessary to manifest. At that moment, I was able to stab him and kill his spirit, forcing him back into the light."

My thoughts wandered to my encounters with Harbinger.

"So that's what makes Harbinger so dangerous, he's been around a long time, and has the strength that results from it."

"I'm afraid so."

We pulled up in front of a Denny's restaurant and I realized I was famished. Going inside, we were escorted to a booth near the window. After the coffee had arrived, I took a closer look at the welt on my mentors face. It was nearly gone.

"Your face is clearing up?"

"The Lord is our healer."

"Guess that saves on medical bills."

He laughed.

"That's one way to look at it!"

"Where did you get the speed you showed in the fight? You were lightning quick."

"That's one of the gifts a Chaser is granted. I know you've been trained to fight, but the Spirit will take it to the next level."

I can take care of myself, but now I've seen the speed of the old man, I'm not sure I could take him.

After we ate, I looked at Buddy, my mind going back to the two run-ins I had with Harbinger.

"Buddy, how old is Harbinger?"

"You mean how long has he been running?"

"Yeah."

"Steve Mason died in the late eighteen-hundreds. He has gone by the name Harbinger, and has been running ever since."

"He's been running for over a hundred years?"

"Yes, but I wouldn't call what he does now, running."

"Why?"

"He's more powerful than most Chasers, and he's more experienced at this than most Chasers ever get."

The fact God had not had someone to take care of Harbinger seemed to irk me.

"What makes him so special?"

Buddy shifted uncomfortably in his seat.

"When a Runner kills a Chaser, which doesn't happen often, he can draw in some of the Chaser's power. It gives the Runner insight into a Chaser, and power to anticipate what a Chaser might do next."

I knew Buddy didn't want to talk about what happened to his mentor, but I had to know.

"Harbinger has killed a Chaser?"

His head went slowly up and down in a nod.

"Two, actually."

"And one was your mentor?"

Again, the slow nod. I felt bad for making him tell me.

"Sorry, Buddy. I shouldn't have pried."

He held up his hand to stop me.

"Don't apologize. I had to tell you eventually, and you need to know what you're up against."

He slowly turned his coffee cup around in circles, staring at the empty bottom, before he began.

"I was three months into my training with my mentor Justin Maddox, when he called me one night to go with him on a chase. Of course, I was ready to go, and met him down at an old warehouse. We sat and waited for nearly two hours until I spotted the Runner. He wore the same clothes then as he does now, black trenchcoat and everything."

I tried to imagine myself meeting Harbinger in an empty warehouse after dark. It's not my idea of a night on the town.

Buddy pressed on.

"Harbinger showed up in physical form, knowing we couldn't cross him over as long as he was manifested. I don't know if he knew we were waiting for him, but he always stays manifested, if he thinks a Chaser could be around."

The waitress stopped at our table and refilled our cups. Buddy dumped powdered creamer in his, and took a sip before continuing.

"Justin had brought his sword but left the cross at home. Instead, he'd brought a knife. The plan was for me to sneak up behind Harbinger while Justin confronted him. I'd stab him with the knife, causing him to return to spirit long enough for Justin to cross him over."

"What happened?"

"Justin stepped out and engaged Harbinger while I slipped around to a spot behind the Runner. As soon as

I was in position, I lunged, and stabbed the Runner in the back. Unfortunately, Harbinger was stronger than Justin had anticipated. The Runner spun, knocked me to the ground with his fist, and retrieved the knife from where it had landed next to me. Justin moved in and thrust his blessed sword, but Harbinger remained manifested, and was uninjured."

Buddy paused, the painful memories etching his face. His voice lowered to a whisper, and his eyes carried a far off look. He was back at the battle.

"Harbinger found the knife, swung around on Justin, and the blade cut across Justin's throat. Justin fell back, and before he could gather himself, the Runner drove the blade into his chest."

I sat quietly, respecting the old man's memory of his mentor. Finally, he looked up at me.

"I escaped while Harbinger absorbed power from Justin. I've hunted him ever since, but I've never got the perfect opportunity to take him down."

"Why didn't you shoot him, why the knife?"

"If you kill a Runner in physical form, he's not crossed over. A gun is not a weapon of spiritual battle, and if he dies, he comes back."

Something else was bothering me.

"Why do you think Harbinger has given me warning not to follow you? Did he ever do that to you?"

He seemed to ponder the thought for a minute before looking me straight in the eyes.

"He never warned me, but he was never afraid of me, either."

His statement stopped me, and it took a minute to register what he was saying.

"Are you suggesting Harbinger is afraid of me?"

I had thought the same thing, but dismissed it as unlikely.

Buddy nodded.

"Not what you are now, but what you will become."

"What do you mean?"

"The power of the Spirit is much stronger in you than in beginning with me or my mentor. I believe Harbinger senses the threat."

"If you're right, why hasn't he killed me? He's had two shots at me, and I wouldn't have been able to protect myself. Both times he surprised me, and I'm no match for his speed."

"You've not committed to the mission. He's being prevented from harming you until you decide."

"How?"

Buddy just shrugged his shoulders. "Some things are not ours to know."

I slumped back in my seat and tried to assess what Buddy was telling me.

I lingered on the idea of trying to explain to Mandy, a cop who fights bad guys all day, there's a whole other world of bad guys she's never seen. She'd probably look at me like I looked at Buddy the first time.

I'd been present, witnessed the reality of it all, and still was having a hard time believing my own eyes and ears. Just the same, it's a calling with few equals. The opportunity to preserve free will for the living.

Buddy was watching me out of the corner of his eye.

"You've made a decision, haven't you?"

Buddy Daniels can be very creepy sometimes.

"Yes, I think I have. I need to spend time in prayer to be sure it's the right one, whether yes or no."

Buddy smiled and stood up. He already knew which it would be.

Like I said, creepy.

CHAPTER 8

That afternoon, after Buddy had dropped me at the house, I decided not to go into the office. Instead, I wanted to take a walk and hash out my thoughts. My favorite way to communicate with God is to walk and talk.

Don't get me wrong, I've got nothing against kneeling in prayer, but I always felt the Lord with me when I walked, my focus on Him.

July was beginning to roll into August, and other than a calendar, there was no way to tell. Both months are hot and dry. After a half hour or so of walking, I reached Endicott Park. It's typical of most city parks with swing sets, slides, and jogging paths. I found a shady spot under a big oak tree and stretched out.

Lord, you know what you're asking, and you know if I'm strong enough, but I need to know inside. Please give me the faith to step forward and accept the mission. I want to be your servant...

****

"Hey mister, you okay?"

I could see the man, and I could feel him shaking me, but I was slow to react. Finally, I was able to respond.

“Yes, thank you.”

I guessed him to be in his early twenties with red hair and an equally red beard. Dressed in shorts and a t-shirt instructing ‘Keep Calm and Pray’, he wore a set of headphones around his neck.

“You were sitting there mumbling something, your eyes wide open. I thought you might have heat stroke or something.”

I got to my feet and looked at my watch. Six-thirty. I’d been here four hours, praying and listening. I was aware of what I’d been doing, but had no idea of the time span.

“I’m fine, but thanks for stopping. I appreciate it.”

“You’re welcome. Have a nice night.”

He put his headphones back on and continued down the jogging path.

I began my walk home, feeling refreshed and alive. God had challenged me to step up for Him, and I wasn’t going to let Him down. I had my answer and all there was left to do was tell Buddy.

Feeling energized, I turned my walk home into a jog.

****

When I got to the house, I found a voicemail from Mandy on my phone. I dialed her number and she picked up on the second ring.

“Hello.”

“Hi, Mandy. It’s me.”

“Hey, Jack. How’s it goin’?”

“Good, you?”

“Better. I got my own car back, which means no more patrol cars for a while, and I’m in the mood to celebrate. You with me?”

I laughed.

"Sure. What did ya' have in mind?"

"Applebee's; I'm buying."

"Sounds good. Let me clean up and I'll meet you there in a half hour."

"Great and hurry up."

"Okay, why?"

"Because I'm already here."

I laughed and hung up.

****

I managed to cut the half hour down to twenty minutes and found her at a table near the back. She looked nice in a teal, sleeveless shirt and black slacks. Her hair was down, resting on her shoulders, curled at the ends. She had a glass of wine in her hand and a bottle sitting on the table. There was more than one glass gone from the bottle.

"Got a head start, I see."

She smiled up at me.

"This is my second, don't worry."

"What makes you think I'm worried?"

She gave me a knowing look.

I've always watched out for her, even though she could take care of herself in most situations. A history of alcohol abuse ran through her family, and she knew I was wary of her slipping into the same pattern. I sat down as she poured me some wine.

Mandy lifted her glass. "To good friends."

"To beautiful dinner partners who pay," I responded.

We clinked our glasses as she rolled her eyes. The waitress arrived, and after giving our orders, Mandy sat back in her chair. She seemed to be studying me.

"Something's different with you lately. What's up?"

I don't make a habit of lying, especially to Mandy, but I couldn't tell her the whole story. Not yet.

"Just feeling good these days. I have work to do and I'm feeling energized by it all."

"That's great. I thought maybe there's a new girlfriend I didn't know about."

I laughed.

"No time for dating these days with my crowded schedule."

I've dated occasionally, and even had an exclusive relationship or two, but nothing lasting. Mandy had always been there to give me advice, or lend a shoulder to cry on, but I'd given up trying to find someone who measured up to her.

Problem is I'm a coward, at least when it comes to telling her how I really feel, and I'm pretty sure she doesn't feel the same way.

Dinner arrived and we ate, tasting each other's entrée, and laughing with our mouths full. When the plates were taken away, I decided to broach the subject most on my mind these days.

"So, I've been offered a position serving in a special ministry. I'm considering it seriously."

Her eyebrows went up as her glass went down.

"I knew something was up! What kind of position?"

"Well, it kinda' ties in with my P.I. work. I find people who need ministering to, and then try to help them. Sometimes, it will take me into dangerous places, but I would be doing a lot of good."

She squinted at me as she does when examining a suspicious piece of evidence.

"Somebody is being deliberately vague. What ministry is it?"

"I guess the best way to describe it would be to call it a 'seek and help' ministry."

Mandy was now squinting so suspiciously I could barely see her eyes.

"Who made the offer? Is it a local ministry?"

"The Lord has brought the opportunity into my path, and I want your opinion. It's here in St. Louis."

I sensed she was relieved find out I wouldn't be moving away.

"What kind of danger?"

"Oh, look who's worried about whom, now?" I grinned at her. "Some of the people I help could be combative."

"Are they mentally ill?"

I laughed. "No."

"I can see you're not going to give me all the details so I'll give you a broad answer to your question. If I had an opportunity to make a difference for the Lord, I would consider it a privilege."

I thought about it for a few minutes as she watched me. I had gone as far as I dared with the subject. I knew she meant it, Mandy never felt she did enough, but like me she'd never found her place.

"I'm sorry to be so vague but I appreciate your advice."

She sat forward and looked me directly in the eyes.

"You know I'm always here for you, right?"

I smiled. It was one of nicest things she'd ever said to me.

"Yes, and it means the world to me."

CHAPTER 9

After dinner with Mandy, I went home and crawled into bed. An hour later, I was still awake and staring at the ceiling. As my dad used to say, it was time to 'fish or cut bait'. I got out of bed and kneeled, my face in my hands.

"Lord, you know me better than I know myself. You have called me to this work and promised to equip me. I don't know what awaits me, but I am willing. I choose to serve you as a Chaser."

I returned to my bed without hearing any great fanfare. There was no heavenly chorus of amen greeting my decision. What I did feel was a peace settling over me, and I slipped into a wonderful sleep.

****

The next morning, I was at Buddy's door before seven. He answered with sleep still in his eyes.

"You're here early. What's the occasion?"

Turnabout is fair play, and at least I wasn't getting him up at the crack of dawn.

"We need to talk."

"Okay, come in. Sarah's putting coffee on."

I followed Buddy into the kitchen where Sarah had put an old-fashion percolator to work. It smelled fantastic.

"Good morning, Jack. Eggs and toast?"

"Please."

Buddy sat down and gestured at the chair across from him. We made small talk until breakfast was ready, and ate in silence, as I made a pig of myself. I'm sure Sarah is reevaluating the impact on their budget of having me eat here. I sipped my third cup of coffee.

"This coffee is excellent."

Sarah looked pleased.

"Thank you. I get the beans ground at the market, and use the percolator. I think it's much fresher."

"I agree. I need to dump my drip maker."

Buddy got up and filled his cup again, but instead of returning to the table, he went to the back door.

"Let's talk out on the patio, Jack."

I thanked Sarah for breakfast and followed Buddy outside. He was standing near the edge of the patio, staring out towards the cemetery. I came up beside him. He spoke without looking at me.

"You've made your decision."

It wasn't a question.

"Yes."

"Are you certain?"

"I am."

"Then we must prepare you."

That's right. He didn't ask me what my decision was, only if I was certain. Remind me not to play poker with this man.

"Tell me what needs to be done," I said.

"There's someone you need to meet. I'll make the appointment and call you this afternoon."

Sarah came out to join us, carrying her coffee and the newspaper. The day was warm, but not uncomfortable, with a slight breeze that rustled the leaves. I could see why they loved this spot.

She didn't look at me when she spoke. "Congratulations, Jack. You'll be in my prayers every day, just like my husband."

She sipped her coffee and opened the paper while I looked at Buddy.

"You tell her?"

"No," he smiled. "She has the Spirit too, Jack."

She was off my poker-playing list as well.

I said my goodbyes and headed for the office.

Despite making the earth-shattering declaration that I would become a Chaser, the day seemed to be pretty much the same as any other. I guess I expected more hoopla, maybe a chorus of angels or something, when I signed on.

Instead, Buddy had acted as if it was a foregone conclusion.

Apparently, I was just the last to figure it out.

****

I parked on the street in front of my office and took the staircase up to the second floor. The usual pile of mail was in the usual place, and contained the usual bills. The one exception was plain white envelope with a hand-written address. It was from Libby Samms.

I dumped the rest of the mail on the desk, grabbed my St. Louis Blues letter opener shaped like a skate blade, and sliced open Mrs. Samms letter.

A brochure of sorts fell out along with a short note. The brochure was from a funeral home. A cross with doves flying around it was on the cover. Inside, I found the information on the funeral for David Samms. I stared at it, startled to see a clients name so soon after a case. I don't usually see death in the lives of people I investigate.

I opened the note, leaning back in my chair.

Dear Mr. Carter,

I wanted to make you aware of my husband's passing. He suffered a heart attack just a day after our meeting at the coffee shop.

I am very grateful for your efforts, which relieved me of any doubt as to my husband's faithfulness.

Regards,
Libby Samms

I took another look at the funeral announcement. The funeral was tomorrow, and I decided to attend, if I could. I wanted to tell her what her husband was really doing at the bar.

The phone rang, startling me.

"Jack Carter Investigations."

"Hi, Jack. It's Buddy."

"Hi Buddy, or do I call you Sensei."

He laughed.

"Call me what you want, but be here at three this afternoon to pick me up. I've arranged our appointment."

"Okay, see you then."

****

At ten to three, I pulled up in front of Buddy's house. He came out immediately and got in. He wore his robe but no cross or sword. I was beginning to think the robe was because he was cold all the time, even in summer. His face bore a fixed, serious expression.

"Turn around, go back to the highway, then north. I'll tell you where to go from there."

I looked at him, decided against small talk, and did as he said. A few minutes after we had turned north, he pointed at a road coming up on the right.

"Turn here."

I followed his instruction, and we headed down a small side street, which dead-ended a half mile down. The entire block at the end belonged to a church.

'Journey Chapel' is as much a chapel as Busch Stadium is a ball field. The place is huge. Manicured lawns, paved sidewalks, and at least six different entrances. A slender spire with a cross at the top, started at the ground, and rose up the front of the building until it touched the sky.

An electronic signboard scrolled service times and scheduled functions in a non-stop neon stream. Under the moving lights sat a small sign, hand painted in an artistic, but simple manner.

Gary Edwards-Pastor.

Buddy pointed again.

"Over there, turn in, and park in back."

I drove around to the rear of the church and parked where Buddy indicated. He got out and I followed. When he got to a small wooden door, he knocked twice.

Shortly, the door opened and standing there was a young man about my age. Taller and thinner than I, he wore a white Episcopalian collar under a black vest. He had close-cropped blonde hair, brown eyes, and a warm smile he quickly displayed when he saw Buddy.

"Brother Daniels, great to see you!"

They embraced.

"Thank you Brother Timmons, it's good to see you, too. This is Jack Carter."

The young pastor reached around Buddy and shook my hand.

"Welcome Jack, nice to meet you at last. Follow me, Brother Edwards is expecting you."

Wait, did he say 'at last'?

We walked without speaking, our feet making no noise, as they landed on the thick purple carpet running the length of the hallway. The dimly lit passage, appearing much older than the rest of the building, was of stone and mortar construction. We walked single file, passing a series of black and white photo portraits, which lined the left side of the passage. When we got to the fourth door, Brother Timmons stopped, knocked twice, and opened it.

We walked into a room the size of my house. Floor to ceiling windows ran the length of the room, light streaming in from the summer sun. Bookcases, made of oak or walnut or some other expensive wood, covered the wall opposite the windows. The shelves overflowed with bibles and books used for studying the bible. The purple carpet from the hallway continued through the door, and stretched to the far end of the room, where a desk the size of a small car, sat in front of a fireplace.

Mounted above the fireplace, a brass medallion nearly four feet in diameter, dominated the room. The picture in the center of the medallion was of a pathway leading into the sun. Around the outside was writing, but I couldn't make out what it said. My foreign language skills are not great, but I guessed it to be either Latin or Hebrew.

Coming around the desk and striding toward us, Pastor Gary Edwards was beaming. Probably in his fifties, Pastor Edwards was easily six three, and a fit two-hundred and twenty pounds. He wore the same collar and vest as Brother Timmons.

"Buddy Daniels, it's been too long!"

They embraced, and Buddy nearly disappeared in the man's bear hug. When the Pastor stood back, he turned towards me, gave me a once over exam, before stepping forward with an outstretched hand. His beaming smile tempered to a grin.

"You must be Jack Carter."

"Yes sir, nice to meet you."

He shook my hand with the grip of a Russian dockworker.

"Never mind that 'sir' stuff, Brother Edwards or even just Gary, will do fine. I've heard a lot about you Jack, and you've been in our prayers."

Suddenly, I felt like the guest of honor at a surprise party, and everyone just leapt out from behind the couch. Apparently, everyone in the room knew what my path was before I did; something I found to be very unnerving.

"I was not aware you had me on your prayer list," I said, shooting a glare at Buddy. "I appreciate you thinking of me."

Brother Edwards reached his arm around me and steered me towards at set of chairs near the window.

"Come, sit, and we'll talk."

Buddy followed us, and all three of us sat in overstuffed Queen Anne chairs. Brother Timmons, who I hadn't noticed leave, returned with coffee and a tray cookies. He handed me a cup.

"Black, right Jack?"

Okay, I was starting to freak out a little. I was clearly known to these men, and I felt exposed, but maybe I was being paranoid. Brother Timmons extended a plate of cookies.

"Shortbread cookie, Jack?"

My favorites. That was too much. I stared at Buddy.

"These gentlemen seem to know an awful lot about me, Buddy. Have you been telling secrets out of school?"

Buddy only smiled as Brother Edwards answered for him.

"Don't be angry with Brother Daniels, he's only been doing what was asked of him. Your name was laid on our hearts by the Holy Spirit, and we've been praying for you ever since."

"When did this happen?"

"About eighteen months ago."

"Eighteen months! You've been watching me for that long?"

"No, we've been praying for you that long. Buddy's only been watching you recently."

CHAPTER 10

After the revelation I'd been on their prayer list for eighteen months, I sat quietly while Buddy and the two pastors caught up on old times. My mind spun with the things I'd learned.

Why had the Lord chosen me?

How are these people connected to each other?

Why are Brother Edwards and Brother Timmons so familiar with Chasing?

Oh, and I had one other question, this one I asked aloud.

"You said 'We've been praying for you', who's we?"

The conversation stopped, and all three men looked in my direction. Brother Edwards stood, walked over by the windows, staring out in the distance.

"Jack, did you notice anything different about this office as compared to the rest of Journey Chapel?"

"Yes. This area seems to be much older construction."

"That's right. This office is in fact the original Journey Chapel. The fireplace was put in when the altar was moved to the new sanctuary, and obviously the pews have been removed, but this is the original structure."

I looked around me at the walls.

"How old is it?"

"This chapel goes back to before Lewis and Clark went west from this city, over two hundred years ago. The new sanctuary was built just fifteen years ago."

He turned to look at me.

"Can you guess why we didn't tear down the old structure when we built the new?"

"Sentimental value?"

Brother Edwards smiled but carried on.

"Journey Chapel was built with the mission of supporting Chasers like yourself. Since its early days, Chasers have come to Journey to seek support, guidance, and weapons. The ministry that takes place in the main sanctuary is a secondary purpose. Chasers and their mission have always been the primary focus of the leaders of this ministry."

He walked back from the windows, sat across from me, leaned forward, and looked me straight in the eye.

"I'm a Counselor, called to minister to those who risk their lives chasing. I've been counselor to Buddy since his decision to follow the path, and if he goes to be with the Lord before me, I will be your Counselor. Likewise, Brother Timmons has been chosen to take my place."

I looked over at Buddy and he nodded his head as if to say it's all true. Brother Edwards sat back, bringing his hands together in one of those 'here's the church and here's the steeple' poses.

"Jack, you asked who *we* are who have prayed for you. It's the three of us here, along with the entire congregation. They don't know what the ministry is, but they know Jack Carter had been called, and had a decision to make. They prayed you would follow God's will."

My mind went to the pictures on the hallway wall.

"Those men in the portraits, they were…"

"…Chasers and Counselors," he finished my question.

I got up and started to pace. Down to the desk, back to the door, and back to the desk. I tried to wrap my head around what he was telling me.

The ministry I'm called to is old, very old, and I'm to be one in a long line of servants. I'd be carrying on a mission that a week ago, I didn't even know existed. Now I'd be stepping into a line stretching back hundreds of years.

I began to understand why the Lord of Hosts himself visited me in my bedroom. Without that visit, I might not believe any of this was real.

None of this information changed the way I felt about my decision. I wanted in, I wanted the opportunity to serve, and I wanted to make a difference. From everything I'd heard, this calling ticked all those boxes in a big way. I stopped pacing, turning to see three sets of eyes focused on me.

"Okay, what's next?"

Brother Edwards got up, walked over to me, put his hand on my shoulder, and squeezed.

"Training. Buddy will finish your training by teaching you more about chasing and how to cross over those who don't want to go."

"And then?"

"Then you come back here for your Anointing Ceremony. The Lord can call you into action anytime after that."

I looked at Buddy, who had a silly grin on his face.

"What happens to you? Retirement and a golden halo?"

Buddy burst out laughing.

"No, not exactly. No golden halo, not even a gold watch."

Brother Edwards squeezed my shoulder again, and with his dockworker grip, it hurt. *I wish he'd quit doing that!*

"Buddy will receive fewer and fewer assignments as you become more and more involved. Eventually, he just won't be called on again, and he can spend time with Sarah. God does not allow a void between Chasers. He calls a replacement to serve before there is a need."

I pointed at the huge medallion over the fireplace.

"What's the significance of that? I'm guessing it has something to do with Chasing."

Brother Timmons got up and walked over by it.

"It's the crest of the Chaser. The pathway to the sun is self-explanatory, but the words are Hebrew. Know any Hebrew, Jack?"

"Anything beyond simple English is a test for me."

Brother Timmons smiled.

"The words surrounding the crest are Hebrew for 'Complete the Journey', the mission of the Chaser."

I tried to remember where I'd seen the crest before. Suddenly, it dawned on me I, and I turned to Buddy.

"That crest is on your sword, isn't it?"

"Yes, and the cross as well."

Complete the Journey. Complete…the…Journey.

I realized these words would become the focus of my life from this day forward, and I was anxious to get started.

Brother Edwards squeezed my shoulder again.

Ouch!

"That's all for today, Jack. Do you have any more questions?"

Uh, yeah. Probably a couple hundred or so!

I shook my head.

"Okay, good. I'll walk you and Buddy out."

I followed Brother Edwards out into the hallway. Buddy was right behind me, as we walked single file, towards the small wooden door at the other end. As we got to the door, I turned to say something to Buddy, and realized he wasn't there. He'd stopped halfway down the hall, and was staring at one of the portraits, tears in his eyes.

I walked back to him.

"You okay, Buddy?"

He nodded but didn't answer. I looked up at the picture.

"Is that your mentor?"

"Yes, mentor and friend. Working with you has brought back a lot of memories. Much of my own apprenticeship has come flooding back."

The man in the photo wore a robe much like Buddy's, but with a hood. His face looked like a well-worn ocean cliff, with crags and fissures, which undoubtedly became even more noticeable when he smiled. A full head of gray hair, which continued down into a manicured beard, surrounded his piercing eyes.

Brother Edwards had come back to stand beside us.

"He was one of the best. Resolute in his calling, even Harbinger didn't scare him. He was one of the few to challenge the runner, who has defined this ministry since day one."

The Counselor looked at me, but thankfully, didn't squeeze my shoulder.

"Brother Daniels told me you've had a run in with Harbinger already."

"Two, actually."

"Really? I didn't hear about the second one."

"It wasn't much really. He surprised me on the front step of my house."

The pastor looked at Buddy.

"He might be the one to do it."

Buddy nodded, wiping his eyes with his sleeve.

"That would appear to be what Harbinger is thinking as well."

I looked from one to the other.

"Hey, I'm just a rookie. No pressure, okay?"

They both laughed and Buddy patted me on the back.

"Okay, fair enough."

****

When we'd said goodbye to Brother Edwards, Buddy and I drove back toward his home, but before we got to there, he instructed me to head in the direction of downtown.

We eventually parked in front of a St. Louis Pizza Palace. Buddy's voice had a far off quality as he pointed towards the building.

"This was an old warehouse before they made a pizza place out of it. That door down there near the south end of the building, that's where Justin and I entered the day we went to face Harbinger."

I could see the door he was referring to, but the warehouse was gone. In its place flashed bright colors and kids enjoying pizza. The night Buddy described was so long ago, but I could tell it was still there in his mind, recreated to include the smells and the pain.

"I came back out that door alone. Brother Anderson, who was Justin's Counselor, showed up to get the body. When a Chaser dies, it must be kept quiet. There can't be any scrutiny of what our mission is, or who we are, so sometimes we're forced to make-up cover stories."

"Like what?"

"My mentor died in a drug deal gone bad. He was supposedly alone. My presence was covered up in the story."

"That's awful. What about his wife and family?"

"He had no kids, and like my Sarah, his wife knew the truth. But his friends and church family really struggled to make sense of it. Many refused to believe the story."

I thought about my mother, and her being told a similar story, if I died on a chase. I didn't want to bring pain like that to her, but I knew if she were told of the calling on my life, she would tell me to accept it. Maybe someday I'll be able to reveal my mission to her. Of course, the best way to avoid hurting her is to not get killed on a chase in the first place.

Buddy seemed to regain himself, sitting up a little straighter.

"He was welcomed into the arms of Jesus, I know that. You ready to go?"

I nodded and put the vehicle in reverse.

A short time later, we arrived at his home. Getting out, he turned and looked at me.

"Be here tomorrow morning. Nine is plenty early enough."

I laughed.

"Okay, I'll sleep in. Say hi to Sarah for me."

He closed the car door and waved as he headed up the walk. I'd just pulled away from the curb when my phone rang.

"Hello?"

"Hi, Jack."

"Hi, Mom."

"How's my favorite son?"

I laughed at the old joke we played out on a regular basis.

"I'm your only son, Mom."

"Okay, my favorite child."

"Only one of those you've got as well."

She laughed.

"Okay, how's my Jack?"

"Good."

"Are you staying busy?"

I thought of her face, and the pain it would cause her, if something happened to me. Of course, my investigator work wasn't without some risk.

"As a matter of fact, I am."

"Great. Have you talked to Amanda lately?"

"Yes. She's fine."

"Glad to hear it. Tell her hello from me. Just checking in to see how you're doing. Gotta run."

"Bye, Mom."

I hung up and drove in silence until I pulled into my driveway. Instinctively, I began scanning for Harbinger. I could tell my senses were already becoming more heightened, more aware of what was out there. I was tuning into spiritual enemies more dangerous than any human foe.

Given what I was feeling, I could only speculate what spiritual gifts were given to an *anointed* Chaser.

CHAPTER 11

I arrived at Buddy's house just after nine, having gone to the office first to clean up some business, and return a couple calls.

Instead of preparing coffee and eggs, as I was getting used to on my visits, I noticed Sarah's car gone. The front door was open, so I called through the screen.

"Buddy?"

"In the kitchen."

I went in to find Buddy in shorts and a t-shirt, filling a sports bottle with water from the fridge. He didn't look up.

"You want some water?"

"No, thanks."

He shut the faucet off and turned towards the backdoor. "Follow me."

"Good morning to you, too."

He ignored my sarcasm, which always unnerves me, and I followed him as he headed for the patio. Instead of going outside, he turned left and started down a small stairway into the basement.

I had to duck to keep from hitting my head, as I carefully made my way down into the darkness. I lost sight of him as he crossed the room, but a few seconds later, I heard a click, and the lights came flickering on.

The fluorescent lights revealed a workout room of sorts. There was the usual equipment such as weights, mats, and a speed bag. However, I hadn't seen some of the other items before in a gym setting.

Leaning against one wall were several lead pipes, three feet long with some sort of wrapping around one end. Next to those were similar plastic pipes, the same wrapping on one end.

At the far end of the room, there seemed to be some sort of track or path, painted jet black, which went up the wall and several feet across the ceiling. I could see dusty footprints along the path.

"Some workout room you've got here."

"It serves the purpose. I know you go to the gym and stay in shape. I also know you've had training in Tae Kwon Do. Fitness and fighting skills will serve you well as a Chaser, but you must refine them, and be able to use them with the power of the Spirit."

"What skills come from the Spirit?"

"Speed and insight. Speed is the physical gift from the Spirit. Insight, an acute awareness of the spiritual world, is the mental gift."

"Both sound pretty useful. How fast will I be able to run?"

"It's not about foot speed," Buddy turned and picked up one of the lead pipes. "You're about half my age, right?"

I nodded.

"Here, take this and defend yourself."

I hefted the half-inch thick, galvanized plumbing pipe. I looked at him with a grin.

"Seriously? What about you?"

He picked up one of the plastic pipes.

"Don't worry about me. Now come on, try to hit me."

I wasn't comfortable with the idea of trying to maim my mentor.

"I don't know Buddy, I mean…"

He moved so fast, I found myself rubbing my thigh, and not knowing why it hurt. He had darted in, struck my leg, and darted back before I could twitch.

"Owww, that smarts! Not bad, but come on, I could kill you with one blow from this …"

Again, he attacked, this time to the side of my ribs, and I just partially blocked it with my elbow. I was going to have a bruise.

"Okay, that's enough old man. You're going down."

I raised the pipe, feinted to one side, and then swung for the other side of his waist. He deflected my blow harmlessly away with his pipe, and before I could regain my balance for another swing, he struck the side of my head. Things spun for a minute, and when I regained my senses, he was standing watching me.

"You're not even trying!"

I'm being mocked by Yoda!

Putting two hands on the pipe, I assumed an attack pose. I was pissed.

Rushing at him, I swung with as much speed as I could. Several lunges and swipes, each one deflected. I stood back, panting slightly, and sweating a lot. He looked like he had just got up from an afternoon nap.

Gathering myself again, I rushed him with all I had, even screaming as a distraction. He deftly stayed just out of reach, deflecting blows, until he lunged back at me. He brought his pipe up over my head, and as I raised my arms block him, he swung his leg under me.

He swept my feet from beneath me, and toppled my body to the mat.His pipe struck me on the on the side of my neck as I went down.

It happened with such speed, I decided against getting up. He'd made his point, and I was pretty banged up.

"Well, that was fun," I said, from my position on the floor.

"The speed you receive from the Spirit is the ability to anticipate, react, and move, with a quickness no human can match. It is not about running fast."

"I can see that," I rubbed my neck. "Actually, I can feel it as well."

He extended his hand and helped me up.

"There's more."

I rolled my eyes. "Great."

Buddy walked over to the speed bag hanging from the wall.

"You ever use one of these in your workouts?"

"Sure, occasionally."

"Show me what you've got."

I planted my feet and started to punch the bag, slowly at first while I got my rhythm, and gradually faster until I had a good momentum. After a few minutes, I grabbed the bag, and stopped its motion. Buddy smiled.

"Not bad. Mind if I give it a try?"

I stepped back, wiping sweat from my forehead, and Buddy took my place at the bag. He closed his eyes for a few seconds before banging at the bag. I've seen professional boxers who were fast, but they weren't even in the same league, as what my mentor was doing while I watched.

His motion was slow, deliberate, but I couldn't see the bag. It was less than a blur, and if it weren't for the noise, I'd think it was some sort of trick. He stopped as suddenly as he started. I was speechless, and when he turned towards me, he wasn't even breathing hard.

"When you allow the Spirit to lead, He can see and move things around you with inhuman speed, yet they appear in slow motion to you."

"What was it you were doing when you closed your eyes?"

"I was giving the Spirit control, getting self out of the way, and asking His leading. You'll be asked to chase people who are bigger, stronger, and faster than you are. Only by harnessing the gifts of a Chaser, will you be able to cross over the toughest cases."

He offered his water bottle to me. I accepted, thirsty and tired. I drank nearly half before handing it back to him. He declined, grinning at me.

"It wasn't for me, I brought it for you."

"Nobody likes a wise guy, I should know."

He laughed and walked over to the path painted on the wall.

"Do you think you could take a run at this, and climb the wall on your feet?"

"I doubt it."

Without saying anything more, he closed his eyes and leapt up the wall, taking two steps before taking two more on the ceiling, flipping and dropping to the floor upright. I was stunned, again.

"How old did you say you are?"

His smile gave away the fact he was enjoying himself immensely.

"You try."

I moved over and lined myself up with the path. Focusing all my energy, I ran at the wall, leaping up with one foot and then stepping with the second. The second never touched the wall as I collapsed in a heap. He helped me up.

"Nothing you've seen me do is relevant to age or experience. It's all about letting the Spirit flow through you, and the Spirit is stronger in you than it ever was with me."

"How do I let it happen?"

"Ask, and get out of the way."

For what seemed like the tenth time, I rolled my eyes.

"Oh, is that all."

He came over and put his hands on my shoulders.

"Sit."

I did, and he sat across from me on the floor.

"Close your eyes and focus on God. Don't think of the wall, only of doing what the Spirit instructs. With your heart, tell the Spirit to guide and lead, and let Him worry about the how."

I did as Buddy said.

"Now, I want to you to stand slowly, maintaining your focus on the Spirit, and face the wall. Do what the Spirit instructs."

I stood for several moments, eyes closed, and praying for the leading of the Spirit. Without making a conscious decision, I found myself moving forward, climbing the wall. One step, two steps, three steps. Next thing I know, I'm lying in a heap on the floor.

"What happened? I was almost there."

Buddy helped me up again.

"You did well, the Spirit had control, but focus under stress takes time. It took me twelve tries to accomplish what you just did on your second."

"Really? Twelve?"

"Twelve, and I thought my mentor was going to lose his mind. Eventually, I learned to get out of the way, and just obey."

He tossed me a towel from a pile in the corner. "That's enough for today."

We went back upstairs, and Buddy fixed us a couple sandwiches. We sat at the table, eating, as he began to talk about faith.

"I know your faith is strong in Jesus and His salvation. You wouldn't have been called if it weren't. What you need to do now is read the stories of Abraham and Moses."

I gave him a surprised look. "I've read them many times, why do I need to read them again?"

"Focus on one thing; Obedience," He sipped his orange juice. "Abraham went in to his wife because God said to. He obeyed, regardless of the probability of a child ever coming true. He focused on what God told him to *do*, not what God said would *happen*." He took a bite and washed it down with some juice. "Likewise, Moses went and told Pharaoh to free the Jews, focusing on what he was told to *do*, not whether the plagues would actually *happen*." He paused while I absorbed what he said. "Obedience to the task."

I was familiar with the stories from the Old Testament, but had never looked at it that way. "So I'm to run at the wall, not worry about how to climb it?"

"Exactly. Obedience allows the Spirit to flow through you, and accomplish the mission you're given."

"And the speed in battle you showed?"

"Same thing. Mine is to go *to* battle, the Spirit flows through me in the combat, and allows me to do things I couldn't *ever* do on my own."

"Why can't just anyone do the same?"

"They can in their own lives and callings, but the gifts of the Chaser, including the ability to sense and see Runners, are given only to those called to chase."

I rubbed my temples.

"How come every time I'm with you, my head hurts?"

"Well, if you defended yourself better, I might not have hit you so hard."

"Very funny, you know what I mean," I stood up. "There's so much to learn."

I started for the door.

"I gotta' go to the office and try to make a living. Same time tomorrow?"

"See you then."

****

Despite being sore from my training with Buddy 'Chuck Norris' Daniels, my afternoon at the office was productive. ICM hired me to watch one of their disability claimants, and two other calls came in making inquiries about my services. I was about to leave for home when the door opened.

"Hello? Anyone home?"

"Hi, Mandy. What brings you down here?"

Her hair was tied up in the usual bun she preferred when working. She wore no make-up, not that she needed any to begin with. She preferred her work to do the talking, not her looks, and I've never seen her on duty in anything low-cut.

"I was following a lead at an office down the street and thought I'd pop in."

Her face scrunched up as if she'd just stepped in vomit.

"Oooh! What happened to your neck?"

I reached up and touched the spot where Buddy had landed his last blow. It hurt, and I flinched involuntarily. I went into the bathroom to look in the mirror. An ugly bruise of green and yellow had formed.

"I did some sparring with a friend this morning. Obviously, he got the better of me."

She'd followed me to the bathroom, and reached up to touch my neck.

"That's awful. You okay?"

"Yeah, I'll be fine."

She withdrew her hand, concern still painted on her face.

"Who's this sparring partner? Do I know him?"

"What makes you think it was a *him*?"

She rolled her eyes at me.

"Let's say I was hoping it wasn't a woman."

"Jealous?"

She laughed.

"No, just hoping my best friend wasn't getting his butt kicked by a girl!" She put her hands on her hips. "So, you didn't answer my question, who is this sparring partner?"

"His name is Buddy Daniels. He came into the office last week. He has a room in his basement with exercise equipment, and he invited me to work out with him."

"Well, tell Buddy Daniels to go easy on you, or I'll have him arrested for assault."

It was my turn to laugh.

"I'll pass that on to him. You want to grab some dinner?"

"Love to, but I can't. I'm due back at the station for a meeting before I can call it a day."

"Okay. I'll walk out with you."

As we got to the street, I caught movement in the alley across the way. Harbinger was watching us, or rather me, and I wondered if he'd been there all afternoon. Mandy nudged me.

"Hey, what are you looking at?"

"Oh, I thought I saw someone across the street I recognized."

She got in her car, which was still in one piece for going on a week, and I closed her door.

"I see your car is still unscarred, how long will that last?"

She laughed.

"No telling! See ya' later."

"Bye."

When she'd driven off, I crossed over to the alley. Harbinger was gone, but the unsettled feeling was still with me. I scanned the entire street but couldn't find any sign of him. Still, the hair on the back of my neck wouldn't lie down.

I crossed over to my car and got in, scanning the street once more with the car mirrors. I couldn't see him, but I can sense he's here somewhere, watching. He's following me, and I need to be careful.

CHAPTER 12

For the next three and a half weeks, I followed the same routine. Sparring in the morning with Buddy, and working in the afternoon on my cases. Saturday was my own and on Sunday, I went to church with my mom. Mandy even came along a time or two.

Gradually, the bruises were becoming fewer, the sparring matches more even, but when push came to shove, Buddy still had the advantage.

"You're not letting the Spirit take control! Follow the lead, and let the Spirit do the work."

Still, I was making progress. My understanding of what I was to do, and what the Spirit would do, increased every day.

On this Friday, my phone rang before five in the morning.

"Hello?"

"Jack, this is your mother."

I tried to focus.

"What time is it?"

"It's early, but I needed to see if you're okay."

"I'm fine. Why?"

"I don't know, just one of those things. I felt the need to pray for you and then call. Sorry to wake you."

"It's okay, Mom. Go on back to…"

Something moved outside my window.

"Jack?"

"It's nothing Mom. I'll call you later."

I hung up and slipped off the bed. Staying close to the floor, I grabbed my gun. On my hands and knees, I crawled out of the bedroom, and around to the kitchen door. From there, I could see the hedge outside my bedroom window, and the man hiding next to it.

There was no mistaking who it was. Harbinger. I stood up, kicked the kitchen door open, my gun aimed at his head,. He spun in my direction, saw the gun, and froze. Judging by the grin, which slowly creased his face, he wasn't frozen in fear.

"You gonna' shoot me?"

"If I have to."

"You know that won't cross me over."

"True, but it'll keep you from trying to cross *me* over. What are you doing outside my window?"

"I've come to deliver one last warning. I know you're training with Chaser Daniels, and your training is nearing the end. Soon, you'll have your Anointing Ceremony, and I'll have no choice. I will kill you."

"You seem to think I have no say in this threat you keep making. Funny thing is I'm not afraid of you. Maybe other Chasers have been, maybe you've been able to intimidate them, but I'm not easily frightened."

As I said it, I realized I meant it. This guy didn't intimidate me like the first time I met him. I knew he could kill me, but I also knew I was getting stronger.

He hadn't killed Buddy, and I was being trained by Mr. Daniels. That fact gave me at least as good a chance as Buddy against any Runner.

For the first time, Harbinger looked slightly unsure of himself.

"It's not too late for you to change this path you're on. Tell Chaser Daniels you've changed your mind."

"But I haven't changed my mind. Now are you going to leave or do I have to persuade you?"

He rushed me with such speed he was hard to see, but I didn't fire the gun. Seeming to float in front of me, his face inches from mine, he growled.

My spirit remained calm, as his eyes bore into mine, and I stood my ground. He couldn't hurt me, not yet, and we both knew it.

Just as quickly, he vanished around the side of the house. Even though I couldn't see him go, the Spirit in me left no doubt, he was gone.

I closed the door and put my away my gun. My heart began to pound as I broke into a cold sweat, much like someone who has done something crazy, then realized what they'd done.

The calmness I felt during the altercation was replaced now by *are you nuts?*

I sat down to keep from falling down.

My phone rang again.

"Hello."

"Jack? Jack, are you okay?"

"Mandy? What you doing up at this hour?"

"Your mother called me, she said you hung up on her, and she was worried about you. She wanted me to drive over and check on you. Everything all right?"

"Yeah, I'm fine. I had a Peeping Tom, but I chased him off."

"Did you get a look at him, we can file a report."

"No, that's not necessary. Thanks for calling, but I'm going back to bed, and you should too. I'll call Mom so she doesn't worry."

"Okay, bye."

I hung up and called Mom.

"Hello."

"Mom, it's me. Everything is fine, and I'm going back to bed now."

"Did Amanda come by?"

"She called Mom, and I told her the same thing I'm telling you, go back to bed."

"All right Son, Bye."

"Bye, Mom. Oh, one more thing."

"Yes?"

"Thanks for praying for me, I need all the prayer I can get."

She was quiet for a moment before answering.

"You're my son. I'll never stop praying for you."

She hung up and I stared at the phone for a minute. If she only knew how much I needed her prayers now.

****

I was late getting to Buddy's for our morning sparring, my alarm was turned off during the commotion earlier in the morning.

"You're late."

"Thank you, Captain Obvious. It turns out I have good reason to be tardy."

"Okay, let's hear it."

"I had another visit from Harbinger."

He pulled out a chair and sat at the kitchen table, offering me the other seat. As had been the norm lately, Sarah was out. I sat down and recounted the events of the early morning encounter. He didn't say anything or ask any questions until I was done.

"You said he seemed unsure of himself for a moment?"

"Yeah, seemed that way."

"I've never seen any sign of fear from Harbinger, not when he fought Justin, nor in the encounters I've had with him. He must sense your lack of fear, the very thing he feeds on, to get an advantage over an adversary."

"He's fast. I was able to track him and sense him, but man was he quick."

"Don't mistake his hesitancy as weakness. He is a most formidable enemy, and every encounter with him comes with grave risk."

"I get it, don't be cocky. I hardly have reason to feel that way, since I've never been in spiritual combat, and he's over a hundred years old. Only a fool would be anything but cautious."

"Wise words. Try not to forget them."

He got up and I followed him down to the training room. He turned the lights on and tossed me my piece of pipe. Buddy had taken away my lead pipe on the second day, when I narrowly missed his knee during sparring, and we've used plastic pipe ever since.

We set up at opposite ends of the room, closed our eyes in prayer, and then began to move about each other. I darted in and landed a blow on his thigh. He lunged back but I blocked his swing for my shoulder.

We switched ends, circling at a distance. He rushed at me with a scream but I barely heard it. The Spirit was in control, an eerie quiet coming over me, as I moved in and out against my mentor.

Buddy landed a blow to my side, but my focus was so intense, I didn't feel it. I responded with two blows of my own, one to the side and one to the shoulder. He stopped, stepped back, and studied me. My movements were fluid, orchestrated, and calculated.

As I watched my mentor, I realized he was breathing heavier than usual, and sweat was beading on his forehead. I had no idea how long we'd been sparring, but I felt completely fresh.

He moved in, swinging at my side and then at my head, causing me to raise my arms to block. Like before, he swung his leg under me, but this time I jumped in the air. As I avoided his leg sweep, I landed a blow on his exposed neck.

He jumped back to his feet and rubbed his neck. A smile slowly creased his face. Without thinking about it, I leapt two steps up the painted path on the wall, three more across the roof and rolled to my feet behind him. I stuck my pipe in his back like a gun. He began to laugh.

Dropping his pipe, he slowly turned to face me. His face beamed with joy as he walked over to me. Enveloping me with his arms, he squeezed me in a miniature bear hug. "Well done! You're ready."

His words brought me out of the battle trance I'd found myself in, and I felt an overpowering joy, and a need to laugh. I laughed until I cried, rejoicing that the Spirit now had the ability to flow through me in a way I never thought possible.

When I had pulled myself together, we went upstairs, and out onto the patio. We drank ice tea and enjoyed the late August breeze, tinged with the scent of fall.

Sarah came home and joined us outside. She bent over and kissed Buddy on the cheek before taking a seat.

"So how goes the training?"

Buddy looked at me and then Sarah.

"He's ready."

She smiled.

"I thought so."

I'm always the last to know.

****

When a big event takes place in life, you're accustomed to seeing friends, family, and well-wishers. Birthdays, weddings, anniversaries, graduations, and such are shared. Those who have guided you, prayed for you, cheered for you, and even disciplined you, are usually present along with gifts, cake, smiles, and pictures.

The Anointing Ceremony was nothing like that. In fact, if it resembled anything, it resembled a funeral. Hushed tones, slow walking, and somber looks were the order of the day.

I sat in the front pew of the Journey Chapel sanctuary on a Tuesday afternoon. Outside, the leaves were beginning to turn and the day was cooler than we'd felt in months. No one who knew me was there. I hadn't been allowed to tell my mother, Mandy, or anybody else.

In fact, the only people in the huge sanctuary were Buddy, Sarah, Brother Timmons, and Brother Edwards. Buddy and Sarah sat in the front pew across the aisle from me. Brother Timmons sat in a chair on the stage watching over a tray covered with purple silk.

Brother Edwards entered from the back of the sanctuary carrying a clear bottle of liquid and moved forward to the pulpit. He nodded at Buddy and Sarah before looking at me.

"Jack Carter, are you ready to receive the Anointing of the Chaser?"

My throat suddenly felt to dry to speak, so I nodded my head.

"Very well, please come up here and kneel at the altar."

I followed his instruction and looked up to see him standing over me with the liquid-filled bottle. He began to pray.

"Heavenly Father, as Jack has heeded your call, and committed himself to serve you in the capacity of Chaser, we anoint him with this Holy Water. We commend him to your mission and your purpose."

The pastor poured the water slowly onto my head.

"May the power of the Spirit and the strength of the heavenly armies be ever at your disposal. May you accomplish your task with honor and faithfulness, never forgetting who you serve, or why you serve."

Brother Timmons came forward with a towel and wiped my face. Next, Brother Edwards and nodded towards the tray. When Brother Timmons removed the purple silk, I could see a sword and a cross, similar to the ones Buddy carried with him.

Brother Edwards took the wood cross first and laid it in my left hand. He poured a small amount of the Holy Water over it.

"Heavenly Father, we bless this cross for the work it was designed for, may it ever be used to return souls to you with peace and joy."

Next, he placed the sword in my right hand. Beautifully made from the Cedars of Lebanon, it bore the seal of the Chaser on the handle. This time he poured the remainder of the Holy Water over the sword.

"Heavenly Father, we bless this sword for the work it was designed for, may it ever be used to return souls to you, be they unwilling."

Brother Timmons stepped back and Brother Edwards indicated for me to get up, the sword and cross still in my possession. When I reached a standing position, Brother Edwards smiled at me.

"Jack, repeat after me. I, Jack Carter, accept the sacred task laid before me…"

I echoed his words.

"…and will faithfully carry out the mission of a Chaser, even unto death."

I finished and Brother Edwards smiled at me again.

"Congratulations Jack, you are now a Chaser."

And that was it. No clapping, no hugging and laughing, just smiles as we walked quietly out of the church. I rode with Buddy and Sarah back to their place where we had a barbecue. Just a normal Tuesday night in early fall. I have to admit, I expected more, but I had no idea the incredible journey that had just begun.

CHAPTER 13

The leaves rustled in a brisk wind, the smell of fall filling my nose. All around me was freshly mowed grass that stretched as far as the eye could see. Interrupting the grass carpet were stones, all in a row.

I was in a cemetery. I could hear the sound of crying, like a crowd weeping in unison, growing ever louder. It continued to grow until I could make out what they were saying.

"David, David, David."

The scene suddenly faded, and was replaced by a hospital room, white and sterile. A heart monitor beeped quietly repeatedly. As I moved farther into the room, I saw a woman sitting in a chair, next to the monitor. She was crying, but I couldn't hear the sobbing, just the consistent beep of the machine.

I watched as the woman stared at the monitor, then closed her eyes. The beeping changed to a long whine, as the line on the monitor went from up and down to flat. As the persistent whine faded from my ears, so did the scene.

What replaced it was a bright light with a lone figure walking towards it. Suddenly, the figure turned away from the path and ran towards me, passing to my right, giving me a good look at his face.

The light flashed, and then disappeared, as if sucked into a vacuum.

I sat straight up in my bed. At first, I looked around for the figure in the light, then for anybody. I was alone in my bedroom, dripping with sweat.

I wasn't positive, but it seemed likely I had my first chase to complete. It's the first person God had called me to return to him and the feeling was one of awe. It'd actually happened; the Spirit was sending *me* to accomplish his work.

The Anointing Ceremony was only two days ago, but Buddy said there was no way to know when the first chase would come. I looked at the clock. Apparently, it would be four-thirty on a September morning.

I decided to write down the vision so I could bring it to Buddy. I needed his help with the interpretation, not to mention a little encouragement. I didn't want to screw up my first mission, even if it turned out to be a simple one.

****

I arrived at Buddy and Sarah's house just after seven in the morning. Coffee was on and both were dressed. I followed Sarah into the kitchen, where Buddy sat at the table, eating eggs. Sarah offered me a plate.

"Yes, please."

I noticed she had extra eggs made already. She carried the pan over and dumped a pile of the scrambled deliciousness onto my plate.

"Thank you, Sarah."

"You're welcome."

She made herself a small plate and joined us. I watched the two of them out of the corner of my eye and neither seemed surprised to see me.

"I almost feel like I was expected."

Buddy sipped his coffee.

"You were."

"Oh?"

"I'm your mentor, and the Holy Spirit revealed to me you had been given a vision. I woke Sarah and we prayed for you."

I could pretend I was surprised they were waiting for me, but I wasn't.

"I wrote down the vision and brought it with me. Can I get your help understanding the meaning?"

"Of course. Eat your eggs first, then we'll take a look at your vision."

****

Forty-five minutes later, we sat on the back deck while Buddy read my memo about the vision. When he was done, he rubbed his chin, deep in thought.

"You got a pen and notebook?"

"I've got my casebook I carry with me. Why?"

"We need to write down what the vision is telling us."

I took out the casebook.

"Okay, shoot."

"In the first part, you're in a cemetery. That means the funeral has already been held. We also know there were many friends and family who miss this person, because of the crowd crying."

I wrote as fast as I could, trying to keep up.

"We learned the Runner is a man, his first name being David."

He looked back at the memo before continuing.

"Part two is the hospital room. What do you think the machine means?"

"Heart problem?"

"I agree, probably a heart attack or heart disease. We also learned he is married, because of the woman in your vision, usually the wife."

I wrote faster.

"What about the third part? I'm sure I've seen his face before, but I can't put my finger on where."

"The third part, with the light and the Runner coming at you, is how you know the vision is real, and not just a dream. The light is obvious, and the spirit of the person turning, is the Runner. As you become more experienced, you will learn to study that moment, and memorize the face going past you."

I tried to think back on that moment.

Where had I seen that face?

It was driving me crazy, which I admit was a short trip these days, but I couldn't shake the feeling I should know who the Runner was. I looked at Buddy.

"What now?"

"Pretty simple, really. You figure out who the Runner is, and cross him over."

"Oh, I see. Easy as pie."

He smiled.

"I said simple, not easy. Read your notes, and organize them, until a picture starts to take shape."

I looked down at what I'd written and started to make sense of it.

"Married man, name David, died of heart ailment. Funeral held, so death probably several days to as much as a week ago. Probably a large funeral with many mourners."

"Okay, what about a physical description, from your brief look at him?"

"Let's see. White, probably mid to late forties, dark hair, and light eyes."

Buddy got up and headed for the house.

"Now, you take what you've got, and start researching funeral notices from St. Louis, then the region, and then the state. Finally Illinois, Iowa, and on out in ever growing circles, until you find your man. The rest you know. Find who they likely ran to, and why, and go cross the Runner."

"How did you ever do this before computers?"

"How did P.I.'s do their job before computers?"

"Legwork."

"Same answer here."

He went through the door, and returned several minutes later, with a new cup of coffee. I was staring at my notes, something nagging at the back of my mind. I reviewed the facts for the twentieth time.

Married, heart attack, forties, and that face. Of course! The funeral letter from Emma Samms!

"I got it!"

Buddy had not yet reached his chair, and turned to face me.

"Got what?"

"I know who the Runner is. David Samms. His wife was a client of mine."

Buddy smiled.

"If we were playing baseball, that is what we'd call a hanging curveball, ready to be knocked out of the park. Now you can do the real work. Find him and cross him over."

I got up and put away my casebook.

"You want to come with me when I find him?"

"Yes and no."

"Make sense will you, please?"

He laughed. He seems to be laughing at me a lot lately, or maybe it's just *with* me.

Yeah, right!

"Yes, I would like to go with you but no, I can't. You're on your own now."

I shook his hand.

"Thanks, Buddy. I'll let you know how it goes."

"Good enough, and may the Spirit guide you."

Oh brother! He even talks like Yoda!

****

I parked the Ranchero down the street from the Samms house. In my time tracking David Samms for his wife, I'd only seen him in three places. Where he worked, the bar where he secretly worked, and home with Mrs. Samms.

The only reason I could come up with for Mr. Samms to run was to reconnect with his wife, to tell her words unsaid, or show her something. I wasn't aware of anyone he'd want to hurt, and the Samms didn't have any children. He had many friends, but they seemed the unlikely target for a Runner.

It took a lot for someone to be a Runner, and it involved strong emotion to accomplish. Since I knew of no one he would hate that much, it figured love was the trigger for his run.

It didn't take long to confirm my hunch. I spotted David Samms sitting on a bus bench across from his home. It took time for a Runner to gain enough power to manifest, and my guess was he hadn't reached that point yet, his spirit still invisible to natural eyes.

I got out of the car, slipped the wood cross over my head, and left my sword in the car. I didn't believe he would be confrontational with me. Since he didn't know I could see him, I walked right up, and sat on the bench next to him. His face expressed his surprise when I spoke.

"What are you doing here, David?"

"How...how can you see me?"

"No fair, David. I asked my question first."

"I've come to tell my wife something before I go."

"That's what I figured. I can see you because the Holy Spirit allows me to. He sent me to tell you what a bad idea it is for you to talk to Libby."

"How do you know her name?"

"It's my job to know."

He got up and started to pace, but I sensed he wouldn't run.

"Why is it bad for me to talk to her? What I need to tell her will make a big difference in her life."

"Oh, I have no doubt about that, but not in the way you think."

He stopped and stared at me.

"What do you mean?"

"Why don't you tell *me* what you were going to tell her?"

"Okay."

He came back over and sat back down next to me on the bench.

"Before my heart attack, I learned my wife had hired a private investigator to follow me. I think she thought I was having an affair, but I wasn't."

"I gather you want to tell her what you were really doing?"

"Yes. I was working an extra job to save money for her anniversary gift. It never occurred to me she would think I was cheating."

I put my hand on his shoulder and stared him directly in the eyes. I could see the anguish he felt over hurting his Libby.

"Listen to me carefully, David. If you communicate with your wife, you prove the existence of the after-life. If she obtains this information, God is obligated to end her time on earth, not because she did anything wrong, but because you would have removed her freewill to choose Jesus or not. Do you understand?"

"I…guess. At least I understand what you're saying but I don't understand how all this spirit stuff works."

It occurred to me David might not be going to heaven. It was pretty clear from what Buddy told me, and from my knowledge of the bible, not everyone I cross over is going to a better place.

Nonetheless, my job here is to cross over David Samms. In all Buddy had taught me, actual rules on *how* I accomplish it, were not part of the lessons. To a person like me, this means I get to make up my own rules, and that was what I was about to do.

"David, I'll make you a deal. I'll deliver your message to Libby, and in return, you'll do what I need you to do to cross over into final rest. Fair enough?"

"Sure, but how do I know you'll keep your word?"

"Because you're going with me. Come on."

I started across the street to the Samms home, and David quickly caught up with me. When we reached the door, I pushed the bell, and stood back. David stood frozen in place next to me, apparently afraid to breathe.

Do Runners breathe? I'm not sure.

Within a couple moments, the door opened, and Libby Samms appeared. She was clearly surprised to see me at her door.

"Mr. Carter? Is there something wrong?"

"No, Mrs. Samms. I received your note about Mr. Samms, and wanted to say I'm sorry for your loss."

"Thank you, but it really wasn't necessary to come all the way over here."

"It's no trouble. The reason I came is because I didn't tell you all I knew about your husband."

David Samms gave me an incredulous look, my connection to his wife dawning on him.

"You're the P.I.? Seriously?"

I did my best to ignore him, as Libby Samms eyes began to moisten, and her hands shake.

"Would you like to come in?"

"No, thank you. I just need a minute of your time."

She stepped outside and closed the door behind her.

"Of course."

"I told you there was no other woman in your husband's life, and that was the truth, but what I didn't tell you is what your husband was doing at the bar he went to. He was working."

"Working? I don't understand."

"David was moonlighting as a bartender to earn extra money."

"I don't understand, he knew we didn't need extra money."

"The money he earned was to buy your anniversary gift. He was going to take you to Hawaii." I paused, letting her mind catch up. "I didn't tell you in my final report because I didn't want to spoil the surprise."

Tears were streaming down her cheeks, but a smile was there to catch them.

"Thank you, Mr. Carter. I'm very grateful to know the whole story."

Not knowing her husband stood directly in front of her, she looked toward the sky.

"I love you David Samms, wherever you are, and I know you loved me," she looked back down at me. "Goodbye, Mr. Carter."

She closed the door and I turned to say something to David when I realized he was gone.

Crap! Crap! Crap!

"Over here!"

I looked over to see David Samms sitting on the bus bench, eyes red from crying. I went over and sat with him, the breeze taking the edge off the warm afternoon. "You heard?"

"Yes," he wiped at his eyes. "What do you need me to do?"

I pulled the cross over my head and showed it to him.

"Just reach out and take hold of the cross."

He looked at the cross, then at his house, and finally at me.

"Thank you."

"It was my honor."

He reached out and touched the cross, light flashed, and he was gone.

I put the cross back over my neck and sat back against the bench. The conflicting emotions of joy, sadness, and pride for my service came together to overwhelm me. I found myself crying and laughing at the same time.

I sat there, and let it all flow, until the afternoon turned into evening. Finally, I looked up at the sky myself.

How was that, Lord? Did I do good?

A peace passing all understanding settled over me unlike anything I'd ever known. I could feel His presence. He was pleased.

CHAPTER 14

The next day, I arrived at Buddy's house full of excitement. It was just after ten in the morning, and I figured not only would he be awake, but finished training.

Sarah's car was still in the drive, but Buddy's white Impala was gone. I knocked anyway.

Sarah came to the door.

"He's not here, Jack. You want to come in and wait."

"You expect him any time now?"

"No. He went on a chase last night, and I never know when he'll get back."

I decided I needed to go to the office.

"Okay, I'll call later. I've got work to do at the office, anyway."

I turned to leave, but she lingered at the door.

"I'm worried."

I stopped. I'd never heard a hint of doubt or fear in any conversation I'd had with Sarah.

"About Buddy? Why?"

"I don't know. Something in my spirit doesn't feel right. I've been praying all night."

It was too soon to panic, and I'd seen Buddy take care of himself, he was probably just finishing a tough chase.

"I'm sure he's fine. I'll check with you in a few hours, but if he comes in, have him call me."

"Okay."

She closed the door and I went to the Ranchero. Sarah being worried meant I was worried. The only person I know, who was more spiritually in tune with God's work than Buddy, was Sarah.

I put it to the back of my mind and headed for the office.

****

After several hours taking care of business and doing research for ICM on their latest case, I still hadn't heard from Buddy. I dialed his number and it went straight to voicemail. I dialed his home.

"Hello."

"Sarah, have you heard from Buddy?"

"No, and I gather by your call, you haven't either."

"No. I've one idea where he could possibly be, I'll run by there, and then come see you. If I find anything, I'll call you immediately."

I hung up, without waiting for an answer, and flew down the stairs to the Ranchero. The St. Louis Pizza Palace Buddy showed me is only ten minutes from my office, and was the only place I could think of to look for my mentor.

Gone was the excitement of the day before, and my first crossover, replaced by a fear for Buddy. I was also beginning to understand how the senses of a Chaser are triggered. My heart was pounding, and as my pulse increased, so did my vision, thought process, and reaction time.

The ten-minute drive took less than seven, but no laws were broken. Pulling up in front of the restaurant, my heart dropped when I couldn't find Buddy's Impala.

I circled the parking lot and drove the alley behind the building. No sign. Just one thing left to do. I headed for Sarah and Buddy's home.

When I got there, the result was the same, still no white Impala. Sarah opened the door as I came up the walk. She'd been crying, and it only heightened my awareness of how serious she felt the situation was. She had her hair pulled up in a hurried bun, and the dark circles under eyes had deepened since this morning. "Did you find him?"

I shook my head and followed her into the kitchen.

"Do you have the plate number for Buddy's Impala?"

"I think so, why?"

"I have a friend at St. Louis PD, and I'm going to ask her for help. Can you get me the plate number?"

"Sure."

While she left the room, I called Mandy.

"Detective Myers."

"Mandy, it's me."

"Hi, Jack. Are you okay? You sound upset."

She knew me better than anyone, including my mother, and she didn't miss a thing. It's one of the traits of a good detective.

"I need your help, Mandy."

"You know I will if I can. What's up?"

"Do you remember me telling you about the man I've been training with at his home gym?"

"Yeah, sure. Buddy something."

"Daniels, Buddy Daniels. He's gone missing."

I could hear her pulling out her report book.

"How long?"

"About 24 hours."

"Jack, you know I can't file a missing persons report on an adult until 48 hours has passed."

"I know, I know. I thought that maybe you could put an all points bulletin out on his car. I just need a direction to look for him, and his car could give me that."

Mandy paused for a moment as Sarah returned with a piece of paper. I took the note, and waited for Mandy to decide.

"Okay, I can do that. Give me the info."

"Thanks, Mandy. You're the best."

I gave her the vehicle description and plate number.

"You owe me dinner for this, Jack."

I spoke the truth when I said, "My pleasure, anywhere you want."

"Deal. I'll let you know if anything turns up. Bye."

"Bye and thanks."

"Anytime." And I knew she meant it.

Sarah's face had new hope across her smile as I hung up.

"Thank you, Jack."

"It's no problem, Sarah. My friend is the best, and if his car is in this city, she'll find it."

"Would you like some coffee?"

"That sounds great."

She busied herself with the percolator while I went down to Buddy's workout room. Everything was as I'd seen it the last time I was there. I looked for notes or photo's, anything that might give me a lead on where he was, but found nothing.

I walked over to the speed bag, remembering the first time I watched him work it. I was amazed, but all he cared about was whether I could be as good at it as he was.

"Coffee's ready, Jack."

"Be right up."

A final search convinced me I hadn't missed anything. I joined Sarah upstairs.

In addition to the coffee, muffins with butter had made their way onto the table. We drank and ate in silence, both us in the same emotional place, worrying about Buddy.

After a while, I refilled my coffee cup, and went out to the patio. Sarah came out with her cup, sitting in the chair across from me. We made small talk and let the afternoon pass. Right now Mandy, and the rest of the cops on the street, were our best hope for a lead.

Of course, every noise from the road in front of the house raised our hopes it was Buddy. It never was, and finally, Sarah went in to fix something for dinner. The sun was going down earlier now, and a chill came to the evening air as October approached. I was about to go to my car, and get a jacket, when my phone rang.

"Hello?"

"Jack, it's Mandy."

"Any news?"

"Afraid not. It's out with all the patrols and they're to let me know if they find anything. I just wanted to check-in."

"Thanks, Mandy. I appreciate it."

"Is there anything else I can do?"

"No, but thanks for asking. I'll probably stay here at Buddy's tonight. I want to be here if Sarah needs anything or Buddy shows up."

"Okay. Talk to you later."

"Bye."

I hung up as Sarah stuck her head out the back door.

"Was that your friend?"

"Yes. She didn't have any news yet. I thought I might crash on the couch, if that's all right with you?"

"I'd like that. Want some dinner?"

I got up and walked towards the back door, passing Buddy's grill. I looked forward to the next time he fixed steaks on it.

****

Dinner, like lunch, was quiet. After cleaning up, Sarah brought me a blanket and pillow to the couch. She retired to her room, and I watched a little TV before shutting it off, opting to pray instead. Eventually, sleep came.

CHAPTER 15

Wind rushed past my face as I soared over barbed wire. A huge concrete structure lay beneath me, divided into sections and overseen by a large tower. The tower was on my left as I soared by, and though it looked like an airport control tower, it clearly wasn't. Everyone around and inside the tower was armed with a rifle.

I came to a soft landing beside an enclosed loading dock. A van, engine running, had its back doors open. Two guards brought an individual in chains to the back of the van, put him inside, and locked the doors.

As the van drove out of the garage, the vision faded to a room with a bed in the middle. The bed looked like a hospital bed, but had two arm supports extending from the sides. Each support, as well as the bed, was lined with leather straps.

The walls were a puke-green concrete, with a large window on one wall. Behind the window sat three rows of people, all grim faced.

I heard a voice declare 'It's time', and some of the people behind the window began to cry. Others turned away.

The scene disappeared, replaced with a brilliant light, and a figure walking towards it. Instantly, he turns and runs from the light. As he runs past, I examine his face. It's a visage pockmarked with scars, and eyes burning with anger.

The light vanishes immediately after the figure runs past me.

I sat upright, confused by my surroundings. After several attempts at making sense of what just happened, I remembered where I was. Buddy's couch.

Rubbing my face to force myself awake, I went over the details of the vision. After finding my casebook on the side table, I wrote down what I could remember.

I knew the concrete building with the tower because I'd been there before. Potosi Correction Center, a large prison at Potosi, Missouri. The room with the bed was obvious enough, I'd seen several death chambers, this one being for lethal injection.

I figured the van to be the transport from Potosi to Pomme Terre. In 2005, Missouri moved executions from the prison to a separate facility at Pomme Terre, Missouri.

I tried to remember the faces behind the glass, but none were familiar or distinct. The face of the Runner was clear however, and I made a rough sketch.

When I was done, I looked at the clock. It was three-thirty in the morning and the vision had left me exhausted. I lay back down and was out cold in minutes.

****

It seemed like ten minutes later when I felt my shoulder being rocked back and forth.

"Jack…Jack."

I opened my eyes to see Sarah standing over me.

"Yeah, Sarah…did you hear from Buddy?"

"No. Your phone is ringing."

I forced myself up and answered the phone.

"Hello?"

"Jack, it's your mother. Where are you?"

I shook my head at Sarah, the caller wasn't who she hoped.

"Hi, Mom. I spent the night at a friend's house…Wait, how did you know I wasn't home?"

"I came to pick you up for church, remember?"

Obviously, I hadn't. Actually, I didn't even realize it was Sunday.

"Sorry Mom, things have been crazy, and I've lost track of what day it is. Go on without me this time."

"All right, Jack. You still coming for dinner?"

"That's the plan. I'll let you know if something comes up."

"Okay. I gotta' go or I'll be late. See you later."

The phone clicked and I looked up to see Sarah holding a cup of coffee out to me.

"Thank you."

"You're welcome. Do you want some breakfast?"

"No thank you, Sarah. I need to go to the office."

"The office on Sunday?"

"I'm afraid so. I had a vision last night so I've got to do some research."

She gave me a knowing smile, tinged with sadness, and nodded.

"I understand. There's more coffee on the stove."

She left, and was in her room when I headed to the office. I struggled with the conflicting desires of searching for Buddy, or going after the Runner in my vision, but I knew what Buddy would tell me to do. I resigned myself to doing the research.

****

The streets of downtown St. Louis are never truly quiet, but Sunday morning was as close as they got. Most deliveries are done during the week and commuters have taken to the suburbs to enjoy the day off. The only bustle comes from tourists going to Arch Park.

The main advantage for me was the lack of traffic, and I made good time driving to the office. Going up the steps, the building was quieter than usual, making for good working conditions. I hadn't seen Harbinger since the night at my house and I hoped today would be no different.

I quickly sorted the mail from Saturday, most of it ending up in the round file, and turned my attention to the computer on my desk.

A few minutes searching and I had the names of the last three men executed in Missouri's death chamber. Clicking on each name gave me a photo, the third photo was my Runner.

The name under the picture was Robert Samuel Gast. A convicted serial killer who was put to death last week. I vaguely remembered the news stories about his trial. Hate was probably the emotion driving him so I'd have to be careful.

I made a list of the people someone like Gast might want to come back after.

Prosecutors

Judges

Witnesses

Surviving victims

Any death penalty case would have extensive reporting and several appeals. A search produced enough information for me to formulate a plan.

I listed the names of two different prosecutors, three judges, and two witnesses. I found one of the witnesses was a victim who survived, and that made her especially vulnerable. My best guess is this woman will be his first mission. Revenge for her testimony, as well as feeling like there's an unfinished task, would create powerful emotions.

Her name is Giselle Franklin from Troy, Missouri. I searched her name, and only came up with news reports from the murder trial. Next, I looked at a map and found Troy, a small town about an hour north on Highway 61. That's where I needed to be.

****

Normally a drive this time of year, like the one to Troy, can be enjoyed for the colors. Late September and early October are one of the nicest times of the year in the Midwest, but not today.

My mind keeps bouncing back and forth between where Buddy is and where Robert Gast would strike first. My mom always told me 'If you try to do two things at once, you'll do neither of them well,' and I'd found it to be sound advice.

I did my best to focus on the task I was charged with right now. Besides, my head tended to pound less if I wasn't attempting mental gymnastics.

Troy is a small city of about ten thousand souls, and I'd printed a map off at my office, before heading out. The drive up took less than an hour, and I got off Highway 61 at South Lincoln Street, stopping at a Fastrip convenience store.

The clerk behind the counter couldn't have been more than a few months over the legal age to work in one of these places. A blonde ponytail tied up in back, and acne covering his face, he was a younger clerk than I'd hoped to find working. I was looking for a local historian type, and this kid was too young.

I used the bathroom before getting myself a large coffee, brought it to the counter, and made small talk.

"Beautiful time of year."

"Sure is mister. That all for ya'?"

"Yeah, thanks. Say, I'm looking for someone. Her name's Giselle Franklin, any chance you know her?"

He scrunched his forehead so tight I was afraid he might hurt himself. Thought process done, he shook his head.

"Nope, doesn't ring a bell. Sorry."

"That's okay. Just a shot in the dark."

I paid for my coffee and started for the door.

"Hey, Mister," I stopped. "You might go by and see Ol' Fred Yeager. He's been around forever."

"Great. Do you know where I can find him?"

"Sure. He spends most afternoons as a greeter up at the Lincoln County Medical Center. Go up to Cherry Street and turn right, the hospital is on the other side of 61."

"Appreciate the help."

"Sure, anytime."

I got back in the car and followed the young man's instructions, getting to the hospital five minutes later. A typical small city hospital, just two stories surrounded by lots of grass and trees.

Parking by the main entrance, I went in hoping to find 'Ol' Fred'. Sure enough, an elderly gentleman with a hospital smock on, manned the front desk. The embroidered name declared 'Fred' was on duty.

Thank you, Lord!

"Can I help you?"

"I hope so. Are you Fred Yeager?"

"The one and only. Who's asking?"

"My name is Jack Carter. I stopped down at the Fastrip, and a young man there said you might be able to help me."

"Oh, that was probably Jeremy. Good kid. Help you with what?"

"I'm looking for a Giselle Franklin. I believe she lives here in Troy, but I don't have an address."

"Giselle Franklin? You have a picture?"

"Not a current one, I'm afraid."

"What is it you want to find her for?"

I'd thought about this question on the drive up here. I needed to answer it without creating a ruckus. Truth is best.

"I'm a private investigator," I showed him my ID. "I've been asked to find her."

"Nothing bad, I hope."

"No, actually it's a goodwill mission."

"Well, the only Giselle I know in these parts is Giselle Taylor. I don't remember her maiden name, but she married Gene Taylor some time back. They live west of the city on Bennington Court."

"How do I get there?"

"Take Highway 47 west through town to Bennington Drive, turn right, and it runs into Bennington Court."

"Thank you very much, Fred. You have a good rest of your day."

"Same to you. Good luck."

The sun was starting to go down as I came out of the medical center. I looked at my map and used my finger to trace the directions Ol' Fred had given me. I was fifteen minutes away, tops. I backed out and headed for Highway 47.

CHAPTER 16

It was almost dark when I turned right on Bennington Drive. I could see where the street dead-ended into Bennington Court, about three-quarters of a mile ahead, and decided to approach on foot. I got out, put the cross around my neck, and tucked the sword through my belt. I covered the sword with my black bomber jacket, which I zipped up part way.

I kept a steady pace, moving quickly without running, and I could feel my senses increasing. My alertness reached an acute level as I got to the intersection of Bennington Drive and Court. I moved across a lawn and ducked below some hedges.

Bennington Court consisted of a u-shaped road with two cul-de-sacs, one at each end. No more than a dozen homes overall, each had a well-manicured, sizable yard. I didn't know which house belonged to Giselle Franklin Taylor, but from my position by the first house on the street, I could see the entire sub-division.

I had the advantage on Gast, who didn't even know I existed, never mind I was coming for him. I didn't know what level of manifesting he had achieved, so I wasn't sure if I found him, whether he would be in spirit or physical form.

I don't know if you'd call it 'Runner radar', but I was quickly aware of his presence, and I spotted him within minutes. He was leaning against a tree, at the end of one of the cul-de-sacs, nearly invisible to me in the dark. His attention appeared to be directed towards the last house on the block, and judging from the fact he stood directly in front of their window, I gathered he was in spirit. I got a charge of adrenaline, realizing I'd guessed correctly, where the Runner would be.

Thank you, Lord!

Moving silently, I was within ten yards of him in just seconds, behind a different tree in the Taylor yard. Taking a deep breath, I stepped out from my cover.

"Gast!"

He tripped as he scrambled around behind the tree he was leaning on. I moved forward as he looked around the tree.

"Who are you?"

"Name's Jack."

"How come you can see me?"

"Call it a gift. I've come to help you complete the journey to the other side."

"I ain't going to the 'other side', as you call it, 'cause I know what's waiting for me."

"Well, not to be disagreeable, but you are going, and you'll answer for the things you did on this earth."

"I suppose you think you can make me?"

Robert Gast is a big man, and spirit or not, he's an imposing figure. I controlled my fear and focused on the task.

Holy Spirit, guide me.

"I can force you, but it would be easier on both of us, if you went willingly."

"That's not gonna' happen, so take your best shot."

With supernatural speed, I sprung off the tree next to him, somersaulted in the air, and landed behind him. I put my arm across his throat, and drew my sword. As I went to pierce him, my phone rang!

My phone? Are you kidding me?

My momentary loss of concentration allowed Gast to manifest and drive his elbow into my stomach. The air rushed from my lungs, and I released him, doubling over in pain.

He took off running but I couldn't give chase. Have you ever tried to run doubled over? It's hard to do, trust me. I had to let him go.

It took me several minutes to catch my breath, and when I did, I looked at my phone.

The call had come from Mandy. I started walking back to my car.

I am such an idiot! I blew the opportunity because I forgot to turn off my ringer! Unbelievable!

I reached the car, got in, and dialed Mandy.

"Detective Myers."

"Mandy, it's me. Got something?"

"We found your friend's car."

"I'm on my way."

****

If you take Market Street due west from the Arch Park, you come to the old St. Louis Union Station. One of the biggest train stations of its day, most of the structure has been converted to a mall, complete with a hotel, Hard Rock Café, and more. The old train platform roof covers the parking lot behind the station. At one time, thirty-two tracks were under this cover, and that's where they found Buddy's white Impala.

It took me over an hour to get back to St. Louis, and by the time I showed up, Mandy was getting impatient.

"Where have you been?"

"Had a case that took me to Troy, a small town up Highway 61."

"I know where Troy is, but I wish you'd told me. I need to have this car towed to the station."

"Towed? Why?"

"We have a man reported missing, over forty-eight hours now, and his car just turned up. It's a potential crime scene."

"Of course, I'm sorry. Did Sarah Daniels file a report?"

"I took her statement a couple hours ago. Nice lady."

"Yes, good as gold. I assume you've canvassed the area?"

"You assume correctly. Nothing."

"So, either he walked from here to somewhere else, or this is a dump site for the vehicle."

I walked over to where the car sat and peered in. No blood, a good thing. No note or clue, a bad thing. Mandy had followed me.

"You look exhausted, Jack. You okay?"

"Yeah, just a long day. You find his cell phone?"

"Nope. No keys or wallet either. Just this."

She reached in and pulled an evidence bag from the back seat. Inside was Buddy's wooden cross. She held it out to me and I took it. I rolled it around in my hands, pretending to have never seen it before.

In reality, the cross told me one very important detail. The chase Buddy was on when he disappeared was going to be confrontational. He knew the Runner was not going to go willingly.

I handed the bag back to Mandy with a shrug.

She grunted. "That was my reaction. I don't have a clue if the cross is relevant or not."

She tossed the bag back in the car as I headed for the Ranchero.

"I'm gonna' call it a night. I'll call Sarah before going home for some sleep."

"Sounds like a plan. I'll call you tomorrow with anything the forensic guys pull from the car."

"Thanks, Mandy. You're the best."

"I know."

I gave her a tired smile and got in my car. On the way home, I pulled out my phone to call Sarah, but it rang first.

"Hello?"

"Jack?"

"Mom! Oh my gosh, I forgot our dinner."

"What happened to you? You always call, at least."

"Mom, I am so sorry. It's been a day from you know where. I was called away to Troy, a city north of here."

"I know where Troy is. What was up there?"

Apparently, I'm the only one who didn't know where Troy was.

"It's a case I'm working on."

"Is everything all right with you, Jack?"

"Yes, I'm fine. Just one of those days. I'll make it up to you, I promise."

"You better," I could hear the anger ebb out of her voice. "I miss seeing my boy."

"I love you too, Mom. Call you tomorrow."

"Goodnight, Jack."

I hung up and dialed Sarah's number.

"Hello."

"Sarah, it's Jack."

"Hi, Jack. Your cop friend was here a couple hours ago."

"Yeah, I know. I just left her. They found Buddy's car."

"They did? Where?"

"Parked in the old Union Station parking lot."

"I gather he wasn't with it?"

"No. Nothing seemed out of place either, so for now we continue to assume he hasn't come to any harm. Detective Myers will keep me updated and I'll be in touch."

"Thank you, Jack."

"Goodnight, Sarah. Try to get some rest."

I hung up and headed home to a few Tylenol PM and my bed.

CHAPTER 17

The next morning, after three cups of coffee to overcome the Tylenol PM, I drove to the office. I didn't know what the day held, but I knew there was research waiting to be done.

I loaded up the files on my computer from the Robert Gast trial, searched the notes, and tried my best to figure out who would be second in line. It made sense Gast would be too afraid to go back to Giselle Taylor's house, so I needed to figure out where he would go next.

What would Buddy do?

I stopped my research, pulled back my chair, and got on my knees.

Lord, hear me please. I seek to do your will and I need your help. Direct your servant, that I may accomplish the task you have assigned me. Amen.

After a few minutes, I got back in my chair. I continued running through documents, comparing names to my list of likely targets, when I found the account of a reporter who was present at the arrest of Gast.

Accused serial killer Robert Samuel Gast, was taken into custody today, without incident. Sheriff's deputies responded to a tip placing Gast at his brother Jeffery's house in North St. Louis.

Robert Gast was found at the home on Emerson Drive, and apparently, blamed his brother for turning him in. As police took the cuffed man out of the house, he screamed at his brother, 'How could you do this? You're my brother!'

Police would not comment on who the source of tip was.

The story went on to tell of Gast's crimes, and when he was scheduled to be arraigned.

I grabbed a phone book.

The news report placed the brother, Jeffrey Gast on Emerson Drive, and the phone book had a 'J. Gast' still listed on Emerson. Revenge seemed likely to be on a serial killer's mind, so my next place to trap Gast and cross him over, had to be his brother's house.

I called Sarah Daniels.

"Hello."

"Good morning, Sarah. Any word from Buddy?"

"Nothing. Anything from Detective Myers?"

"Not yet, and it'll probably be this afternoon before the forensic report on the car is ready. I'm going to talk to Buddy's Counselor and see if he has any idea where Buddy might be."

"You're talking about Brother Edwards, I don't have his number, or I would have called him."

"I'll go see him and let you know if he has any info. Bye."

I hung up and headed for the car. I needed to stake out the Jeffrey Gast house, but first I wanted to see Brother Edwards.

****

I arrived at Journey Chapel just before noon. The church campus was ablaze with fall colors, and a light breeze moved the leaves in a way that made them shimmer.

I parked around back and went to the small wooden door I had first seen with Buddy. I knocked twice, and Brother Timmons soon appeared at the door, swinging it wide for me to come in.

"Brother Carter, nice to see you. To what do we owe the pleasure?"

"I'm not on a casual visit, I'm afraid. Is Brother Edwards here?"

It seemed the clergyman sensed my mood, because he closed the door, and started down the hallway.

"Come with me."

We walked down the old passage, and I couldn't help taking a second look at the portrait of Justin, Buddy's mentor.

Did Buddy meet the same fate as his mentor? Death at the hands of Harbinger?

I blocked the thought, and followed Brother Timmons into the large office.

Pastor Edwards sat working at his desk, the fireplace crackling behind him, and smiled widely when he saw me.

"Jack, what a pleasant surprise."

"Hello, Pastor. I hope I'm not intruding, but I have a situation."

He got up and came around the desk, shaking my hand, and steering me toward a couple chairs.

"Don't ever think twice about coming here. We're here for you and your mission. What's the situation?"

"Have you heard from Brother Daniels?"

The two clergyman exchanged glances.

"No, why?"

"He's been missing for three days."

"Three days? Was he on a chase?"

"Sarah said he was, but she expected him back by now. Last night, we found his car."

Brother Edwards stood up and started pacing, rubbing his chin as he talked.

"Obviously he wasn't with the car."

"No, but I did find his blessed cross. The sword was gone."

"Where was the car found?"

"In the parking lot behind the old Union Station."

The Pastor stopped abruptly, looking at his assistant. I watched as an unspoken understanding passed between them. I wanted to be included.

"What? Does Union Station mean something to you?"

Brother Edwards restarted his pacing, slower now. His words came slowly, too.

"Brother Daniels has had several run-ins with Harbinger, most brief and unplanned, but the one place he nearly trapped the old Runner was near Union Station."

I had avoided bringing the suggestion of Harbinger's involvement into the search for Buddy, partly because I had nothing to suggest it, and partly because he was the one individual I didn't want to confront just yet.

"What happened?"

"There was a confrontation, Buddy getting the upper hand, but he couldn't inflict enough injury to force Harbinger to return to spirit. Eventually, Buddy tired and Harbinger ran."

I followed the slow march of the Pastor with my eyes, as he went from one end of the room to the other. My phone ringing startled all three of us. I gave a shrug as an apology to the two Brothers and answered it.

"Hello."

"Jack, it's Mandy."

"Hey. You get the report back?"

"Yes, and there was nothing. No blood, no unidentified fingerprints, nothing."

"Okay, thanks." I couldn't hide the disappointment in my voice.

"There's more."

"More?"

"I got copies of the security tapes from the mall cameras. They show Buddy Daniels driving into the lot, parking, and leaving. Another camera picked him up at an exit, crossing 18th Street."

"Mandy, that's great. Anything else?"

"No, but I've got officers canvassing the area east of Union Station."

"Okay, let me know what you find."

"Will do, bye."

I hung up and turned towards Brother Timmons. "Do you have a city map?"

"You won't need it," It was Brother Edwards, who apparently heard both sides of my conversation with Mandy. "I can tell you where he went."

"You can? How?"

He'd stopped pacing, instead staring out the large bank of windows.

"The confrontation I was telling you about, between Brother Daniels and Harbinger, took place in the Federal Post Office building just east of Union Station. The third floor was used for storage, and it was there that Buddy surprised Harbinger."

"And you think he was trying to do it again?"

"I don't know, but I would bet that's where he was going."

I got up and moved towards the door.

"Thank you, Pastor. I'll let you know what I find."

"Jack."

I turned back to face the Counselor.

"Yes?"

"He's still with us."

"Buddy?"

"Yes. The Spirit is telling me he's still alive."

"I know, I'm getting the same message"

"But Jack."

I frowned, impatient to get going.

"Are you on a chase of your own right now?"

"Well, yes actually."

"I know you want to find Buddy, but your first responsibility is to the chase. Leave Buddy to the Lord, and do what the Spirit has called *you* to do."

I hesitated, wanting to argue the point, but I knew he was right. Mandy is looking for Buddy, and I need to go to the Gast house before the Runner does irreparable damage.

"I understand, Counselor."

He gave me a small smile and nodded his head.

"We'll be in prayer for both of you."

I headed out the door and down the hall.

CHAPTER 18

I arrived at the Jeffrey Gast home just as the sun started down. Judging from the vehicles in the driveway, two SUV's, it was a good bet both Jeffrey and his wife were home.

The neighborhood was a typical middle class construction project. Cookie-cutter houses built all in a row, windows and doors in the same location, both sides of the street. The only thing to set one house from another was landscaping and paint.

The Gast home sat in the middle of the block, its backyard surrounded by chain link fence. Unfortunately, I didn't see any evidence of a dog. I was hoping Jeffrey had a pet who might give me a heads-up if a spirit was around.

Animals, dogs in particular, are very aware of any spiritual presence. I asked Buddy why he didn't have a dog, given the advantage he might gain from having a four-legged alarm.

"Actually, I've always wanted a dog, but not just any dog will do for a Chaser."

"Really, why's that?"

"Most dogs can sense the presence of a spirit, and most dogs will snarl or bark, which is great if you need a warning. However, not all dogs have the ability to discern the difference between good and evil, friend or foe. The sense of when to alert and when to be quiet is what would make a dog truly valuable to a Chaser."

"Does such a breed exist?"

"I understand some Chasers have found a canine companion. It's not a particular breed though, but a *type* of dog. It must be in tune with your spirit when on a chase. I've heard of German Shepherds, an occasional retriever, even a Chihuahua."

"A Chihuahua? That's a pocket pet!"

He'd laughed, and as I remembered his smile, I had to force myself to stay focused. I fought the urge to abandon the stakeout and go look for him. I hadn't been able to sense Gast was here yet, but I needed to stay put.

I felt the vibration of my cell phone in my pocket. Yes, I remembered to turn off the ringer!

"Hello."

"Hey, Jack. It's Mandy."

"Hi, Mandy. Any news on Buddy?"

"Afraid not. My guys canvassed a three block area around Union Station with no luck."

"What about the post office across 18th?"

"Yeah, nothing. Why?"

"One of Buddy's friends mentioned the post office as a place Buddy sometimes went. Have you called Sarah Daniels?"

"Yes, I gave her an update about an hour ago. What's doing?"

"I'm on a stakeout. Do you want to join me?"

"Gee, that sounds like fun, but my waistline couldn't take it."

It's well known among cops and P.I.'s alike, that stakeout duty is calorie duty. Eating passes the time, and sitting adds the pounds. Stakeout equals unwanted added weight.

I laughed at her. "Your waistline could be on a month-long stakeout and you'd still be trim."

"Thank you sir, but the answer is still no. By the way, you owe me dinner."

"I haven't forgotten, just too busy to pay up right now."

"Okay. Talk to you later."

I hung up. Of course, I knew she wouldn't join me, or I wouldn't have asked. Can't bring her on a chase, even if she would be great at it.

I hunkered down in my seat, watched, and waited.

****

I jerked awake in my seat. I don't know how long I was out, but the last time I remembered looking at my watch was one in the morning. I looked again, three-thirty.

I got out of the car, reached into the back seat, and found my thermos of coffee. I poured the remaining few swallows into my mug while scanning the neighborhood. Nothing seemed amiss and I still had no sense of Robert Gast. All the houses were dark, with only an occasional dog barking to break the quiet.

Frustrated, I tossed back the rest of the coffee, and threw the thermos back in the car. I wasn't getting anything accomplished here and Buddy was still missing. I started the car and headed for Union Station.

****

The streets of a big city are never really empty. I know the movies will show a situation where a main city street is deserted, which is great for movie plots. In real life, people and vehicles are moving around a city at all hours.

Delivery trucks, taxicabs, police officers, newspaper delivery people, and just ordinary folks out too late. When I got to the post office near Union Station, I parked on Market Street, took out my sword, and locked up the Ranchero. I walked around the large building, looking for an entrance where I might not be observed. One of the busiest places, especially in the early morning, is a large post office. The mail needs to be dropped, sorted, and prepared for delivery before your local guy or gal can come to your door.

This made finding a way into the post office nearly impossible, even at night. There is an old steel fire escape, as I'd hoped, but the ladder to the ground floor was retracted. Still, it might be a way in.

I was just about ready to leave when my senses stopped me in my tracks. There's a Runner in the area, and not just any Runner, this one is strong. I couldn't be sure if I was getting the feeling from the post office building, or somewhere else nearby.

Unfortunately, a Chaser can't pick up if another Chaser is in the area. Naturally, I suspected Harbinger is the Runner I'm feeling, but I've got no way of knowing if Buddy is with him, or where exactly they might be.

A look at my watch told me I would see the sun soon. Six in the morning and traffic was picking up considerably. I needed food, and to get back to my stakeout, but I was coming back in the late afternoon to find a way up to the third floor.

Even though I couldn't sense Buddy, my gut told me Harbinger was holding him, which in turn made me a little queasy. I returned to my car and went to find something bland to eat.

Facing Harbinger seemed now to be inevitable and I felt less than prepared. The Holy Spirit, however, was more than ready. He just hadn't told *me* yet.

Like I said before, I'm always the last to know.

****

I made it back to the Gast neighborhood around seven-thirty. Both vehicles were still in the driveway, and I still didn't sense the Runner.

One thing I'd forgotten to ask Buddy during my training was how these Runners get around. For all I knew, Robert Gast was walking from Troy(a small town north of St. Louis!) to his brother's house. I tried to do the math in my head, how long it would take him walking to get here, but I was too tired. When I see Buddy again, I'm going to have to ask him about Runners, and their method of travel.

The street was waking up and people were going to work. The last wisps of summer were still around and I found myself looking at the colors on the maples and oaks.

Did I mention my concentration tends to wander? Not a strong character trait of a P.I., but I usually overcome it with patience. Anyway, I was marveling at a beautiful red maple when my heart started to pound. He's here.

I slipped down in my seat a little and tried to keep from being spotted. I knew if he saw me, he would bolt. Secrecy was not one of my weapons now, but I could still surprise him by stealth. I also had to consider the possibility he may be carrying a weapon.

It took less than two minutes to spot him. He jumped the fence into his brother's backyard, and was moving toward the back door. I got out and moved quickly to the other side of the house, sliding along with my back to the wall, until I could see into the backyard.

The serial killer was in physical form, probably so he could carry the piece of metal pipe in his hand. It took just one look out the window by someone in the house to ramp up the situation. If it's just brief, and I cross the Runner over quickly thereafter, the people will put it down to seeing things.

But if Gast is able to attack someone, injure someone, or talk to one of them, it won't matter how fast I cross him over. Those people will be taken. I had to move now.

I stuck my head around the corner once more and Gast was coming towards me. Apparently, he hadn't found a way inside, and was coming around the side where I was. I ducked behind a bush in the neighbor's yard.

I had my sword drawn, and watched as he came through the metal gate creeping toward the front of the house. When he got past my position, I launched myself at him, hitting him with a football block to his back.

At the last second, he sensed me, and rolled slightly to one side. He hit the ground with me on top of him, but slipped out from under me, and made it to his feet first. The metal pipe came swinging down, aimed for my head. I tried to block the blow and it struck me on the forearm. Pain flashed through my brain as my arm began to throb.

He lost his balance, the force of his swing tipping him forward, and I drove my foot into his knee. He howled and fell in front of me. My injured arm was of little use, but I scrambled behind him, and wrapped my good arm around his throat. He kicked up and down as I did my best to keep the pressure on his windpipe.

The effort to fight me was taking its toll and he began to return to spirit. When he started to lose consciousness, his physical manifestation left him completely. I forced my weak arm to take hold of the sword and thrust it into Robert Samuel Gast. With a flash, he was gone.

I collapsed backward, pain flaring as my arm hit the ground. I lay gasping for oxygen until I forced myself to get up and make my way back to the Ranchero. I didn't want to answer any questions to the neighbors.

I contemplated where to go. It was clear I needed medical attention, but a hospital meant questions, as did calling Mandy. There was one person I knew could doctor me, and honor my need for secrecy. I fired up the Ranchero and headed for former nurse, Annie Carter.

CHAPTER 19

By the time I got to my mother's house, my arm was turning three shades of purple. It throbbed and any movement sent pain shooting into my shoulder.

I parked in the street and made my way to her door. Rain clouds were moving in and a cool wind from the north caused dropping temperatures. It felt like the first cold rain of fall was coming.

I tried the door, it was locked, and getting my keys back out of my pocket was too painful. I rang the bell.

When she opened the door, she didn't see my arm, but she could tell something was wrong.

"Jack, what is it?"

I looked down at my arm and her gaze followed mine.

"For Heaven's sake, what happened? Get in here."

She opened the door wide for me to come in, paused to look outside as if the person responsible for my arm might be following, and shut the door.

"Did you drive here?"

"Yeah."

"What happened?"

"Attacked."

"By what, a Yeti?"

It was funny, but it hurt to laugh, so I kept it to a smile.

"No. A man with a pipe."

She steered me to a chair in the kitchen and sat me down.

"Rest the arm on the table where I can get a better look at it."

I did as I was told. "Could I have a drink of water?"

She went to the cupboard and got a glass, filled it with water, and grabbed some pills from the counter.

"Here, take these."

I knocked back three aspirin and drained the glass. She got me a refill and turned her attention to my arm.

"This is gonna' hurt."

My mother is not usually one for understatement, but saying this will hurt, is like saying a bullet wound stings. She manipulated my arm, probed the bone, and in the process, made me cry.

"I don't think it's broken, but I can't be sure without an x-ray. We'll take you to the hospital."

"No. I came here because I didn't want to go to the hospital. Is there anything you can do?"

Despite giving me her best 'don't be ridiculous' look, she could see there was no point in arguing.

"It's a deep tissue bruise, and probably a bone bruise. I can sling it, put ice on it for the swelling, and watch for signs of it deteriorating. If the wrist starts to swell, you'll have no choice. It'll be the hospital or lose it."

"Okay. Fix me up for now, please."

"Very well, but I'm not on board with this plan."

"I know. Thanks anyway."

****

It took a little over an hour for her to get me taken care of and sitting semi-comfortably in my dad's old recliner. The ancient Lazy-boy was still in decent shape and Mom had refused to get rid of it. It was a relief to be resting, and the ice plus Tylenol was taking the edge off the pain.

I was just starting to doze off when I heard the doorbell. Mom went and answered it, returning a minute later with Mandy in tow. Mandy was in her detective clothes and her expression, as she came around the corner, told me more than a mirror could.

"Jack!"

I gave her a half-smile.

"Hi, Mandy. What's shaking?"

She sat down in the chair next to me and touched my good hand.

"Annie called me. She said you were attacked by a man with a pipe?"

I scowled at my mother. Even though it was nice to have Mandy holding my hand, I had hoped to avoid the questions she was sure to ask.

"Yeah, afraid so. Gave me a pretty nasty bruise on the arm."

"What happened?"

"I was on the stakeout I told you about, when a guy took exception to me being there, and used the pipe on me."

"Who was it? Can you give me a description?"

"Not really. He came and went almost like a ghost."

"Well, we can still…"

I cut her off.

"No, please. No reports, no investigation."

Mandy stared at me, frustration etching her face, wanting to argue. She noticed she was touching my hand, withdrew it, and sighed.

"Can I change your mind?"

"Nope. I just want to rest."

"Fine, have it your way."

I gave her another half-smile and passed out before I could ask about Buddy.

****

Well, it turns out the aspirin, which is what I thought my mother gave me, was something else. Three days after arriving at Mom's door, she finally let me come around.

"How long was I out?"

"Three days."

"Three days! What did you give me?"

She was unfazed by my outrage.

"Percocet."

I tried to push myself up, forgetting about my arm, and pain shot into my shoulder.

"Ow, ow,ow!"

"Oh, stop being such a baby. Your arm is healing up nicely. It went from purple to green to yellow, but the wrist didn't swell. It's unlikely you have a break."

I sat up, more carefully this time, and tried to clear my head.

"Any news on Buddy?"

"Amanda, who has stopped by every day, said there's nothing new."

The news didn't surprise me. Somewhere in my drug-induced fog, I had concluded Buddy was safe, or at least still alive. It seemed likely to me Harbinger was using my mentor to lure me into a confrontation. I had every intention of obliging him.

"Mandy stopped by each day?"

"She did. If you ask me, that girl loves you."

"It may seem that way, but we've been friends a long time, and there's never been any romantic involvement."

"Why not? Don't you like her?"

How did I get into this conversation with my Mom?

"Well, yes I like her, but it's never been that way."

"Don't see why not?"

"Can we talk about something else?"

"Okay, like what?"

I looked down at myself. I was in Dad's old pajamas, upstairs in the guest room, in bed.

"How did I get changed and into this bed? Don't tell me Mandy helped you!"

"No, of course not. Mr. Danzig next door helped me."

I started to test my arm, and despite some soreness, it seemed to be in relatively good shape.

"Thanks for taking care of me, Mom."

"What are mothers for? You're welcome. You hungry?"

"Starved. Where's my clothes?"

"In the closet. I'll see you downstairs."

After dressing, and polishing off a double helping of Mom's famous biscuits and gravy, I got in the car and headed for Journey Chapel.

****

Brother Timmons let me in to the office where Pastor Gary was waiting for me.

"Jack, good to see you. I heard you'd got yourself banged-up pretty good, was it a Runner?"

"It was. I succeeded in crossing him over but not before he got a solid blow in. How did you find out?"

"Sarah Daniels called and let me know."

The mention of Sarah reminded me I needed to call her. Mandy must have kept her in the loop.

"Do you still sense Buddy Daniels?"

He sat back down behind his desk, crossed his hands, and studied me.

"I do, but he's weaker than before."

"Okay, late this afternoon, I'm going after him. I'm pretty sure Harbinger is using Buddy as bait."

"Bait for what? You?"

"Buddy said Harbinger wants me out of the way. I think he's waiting for me to come after Buddy."

"That would mean it's a trap."

"Only if I was unsuspecting, but I'm not. I'll be careful."

"Where do you think he is?"

"Post office, as you suggested."

"What can we do?"

"Pray. I know Harbinger is stronger than I am, but I have God's Spirit. I need your prayers."

He got back up and came around the desk, putting his hand on my shoulder.

"I'll gather together a prayer team, they won't know what the prayers are for, but they'll know someone is on a mission."

"Thank you. I'll be in touch."

****

I went home before heading down to Union Station. My plan was to park where Buddy had left his car, then move to the back of the post office during the slowest time of the day.

Mail carriers will have come back in from their routes but the truck deliveries of the next day's mail won't have started. I should be able to get into the building unnoticed.

I showered, dressed in my usual outfit of black and white, pulling on the black bomber jacket. Before I put the jacket on, I took some gauze and wrapped my sore arm repeatedly until it had a type of forearm pad. I wrapped that in duct tape. I didn't want the pain to be any more distracting than necessary, if the arm was hit.

My sword would go through my belt as usual, but this time I packed a knife. The power in the sword was to cross over a Runner, but the knife gave me something to defend myself with, if we went hand to hand.

It was just past five-thirty when I got in the Ranchero and headed for downtown. The ride would be easy because I was going against the flow. Most people were trying to get out of the city and I was headed in. I sipped a coffee and pulled onto the freeway.

My senses were already getting fired up, and I could tell I was as ready as I could be, given my limited experience. I encouraged myself by remembering that I may not have been a Chaser long, but I'd been a good P.I. for years. The skills I'd acquired from doing that job would certainly help me in the new one. At least it sounded good.

CHAPTER 20

The sun was beginning its descent into the western horizon when I parked in the old covered train yard. I got out and slid my sword into my belt. My knife was in my back pocket and I'd remembered to bring a flashlight.

I thought of Buddy and wondered if I was retracing his steps from the night he disappeared. If I was, hopefully with a different result.

I wanted to approach the post office from the back. I crossed Market Street to north of my position, walked east two blocks, and re-crossed Market to an alley, which led down to the back of my destination.

I arrived at the old fire escape, my senses telling me I was in the right place. A Runner is close and my nerves told me it was Harbinger. After picking my path, I took three steps, launched myself up the building wall, and landed on the second story fire escape landing.

Hunching down, I waited a full five minutes, making sure I hadn't aroused suspicion. Nothing but the sounds of late evening traffic. Slowly, a single step at a time, I made my way up to the third floor landing. Waiting again, I made sure I was undetected to the people below.

Finally, I tried the fire exit door. Locked.

Harbinger would know I was in the area, he'd obtained the ability by absorbing some of Justin's power when he killed him, but it was far less sensitive than the Spirit in me.

A Chaser can sense when contact with a Runner is imminent, and avoid what could be a fatal encounter, by reacting at the last minute. Harbinger would know I'm in the area, but not where I was, and I would have warning if he launched an attack. I just hoped it did me some good. It doesn't do much good to know a train is coming if you're stuck in the middle of a tunnel!

I surveyed my options, and decided I could get in through a partly open window. I dove for the windowsill, grabbing on with my good arm, and steadying myself. I held on with one hand while pushing the window silently open with the other. As sore as my arm is, it was clear the Spirit was giving me strength.

Not able to see anything, I pulled myself into the window, and onto the floor. Any light still available outside was lost in the building. I snapped on my flashlight.

As the beam played around the room, I found myself in some sort of closet. Maybe eight feet away, a door into the main floor area sat closed. The third floor of the building was apparently still undergoing renovation, and construction equipment was the only stuff in the room. With as little noise as possible, I crept to the far end of the room, and tried the doorknob. It turned easily. I left the door closed and listened.

Five or ten minutes went by before I was confident I hadn't raised an alarm with the people below. Turning the doorknob until I felt the click, and the door came free, I pulled it slowly open a crack. I could see the rest of the floor, and surveyed the situation.

Blue neon lights from the Union Station sign glowed through the windows, giving the room an eerie luminescence, and making some vision possible now that the sun was down. My heart stopped when my eyes settled on a table in the middle of the room.

A small figure lay tied to some sort of workbench, with what looked like ratchet straps across his ankles, waist, and chest. It had to be Buddy, and he wasn't moving. His face was turned away from me, so I couldn't tell if he was conscious or not. I wanted to rush over, cut him free, and bail out. I knew better.

I took a deep breath and forced myself to look from one corner to another, searching the pale, blue light for any sign of Harbinger. The floor was being divided up into offices. Steel framing had been raised across the area and I could make out where doors would eventually be.

Tools, pipe, and wire were strewn around the entire worksite. If workers were here during the day, then Harbinger must have been moving Buddy, and bringing him back after they'd gone home.

He'd gone to a lot of trouble to get me here, but where was he?

There was a moan, and Buddy's head rolled in my direction. His mouth was covered with duct tape and he still had the clothes on he was wearing when he went missing. His face showed the exhaustion from his ordeal and a tinge of guilt came over me. He was in this situation because of me.

I waited ten minutes more, every sense on alert, but I couldn't locate Harbinger.

Maybe he's looking for me to come in another way? Maybe he's watching the regular stairway?

Finally, there appeared to be no choice but to try to free Buddy, and get out of there. Harbinger didn't seem anxious to reveal himself and neither Buddy nor I have all night.

Flipping my flashlight on, I drew my knife, and moved swiftly to Buddy's side. As I began to cut at the strap across his chest, his eyes popped open. It seemed at first he didn't recognize me, but suddenly his eyes got wide, as if he knew who I was.

The next few seconds were a blur. My thoughts and actions became quick, anticipating everything.

Buddy's eyes aren't big because he's recognized me, he's staring past me to the ceiling!

I lurched to one side, avoiding the main blow, as Harbinger dropped from the ceiling.

You idiot! You didn't check the ceiling!

A large, black boot landed on my sore shoulder sending pain rushing through my body.

Knocked to the floor, I managed to ignore the pain, and leap back to my feet. A leg sweep took the feet from under Harbinger. He fell against the workbench, sending it careening across the room with Buddy on it.

Harbinger was up and growling. He came back at me in a flash, landing a solid kick to my chest. I landed on my butt and slid backwards along the cement until a steel post stopped my progress.

Big and Black came towards me, knowing I was temporarily stunned, and went to kick me again. This time I gathered myself, dodged his kick, and plunged my knife into the top of his planted foot. He howled and fell back, jerking the knife out of my hand.

It bought me enough time to collect myself, and look for another weapon. A piece of metal pipe found my hand, and as the Runner came towards me again, I ran to the wall, up onto the ceiling, and dropped down behind him.

Apparently, he'd seen this one before. When I dropped to swing the pipe, he landed a straight right to the end of my nose. Blood gushed from my face as I staggered backwards, crumpling against the far wall.

I could barely see over my swollen nose, but Big and Black is hard to miss, and he was moving in to finish me off. I frantically looked for something to ward him off with, but there was nothing. He had slowed to a limp now, his foot still sporting the protruding knife, his face grimacing.

Well, at least if he kills me, he'll know he's been in a fight.

I reached back to the wall to push myself up, when my hand fell on a thick piece of wire. I looked up to see where the wire went, saw the electrical junction box, and probed for a switch. As Harbinger got to me, I found the central switch, pulled it, and lunged out with the chunk of wire in my hand.

The bare end of the wire struck him in the groin, and he began to scream. Blood made it hard for me to see, but his advance had stopped, and he seemed frozen in place.

For what seemed an eternity, but was probably only seconds, Big and Black was suddenly orange and white. The orange of the sparks with white of his face made him much less intimidating. More importantly, he began to shimmer, his manifest state reverting to spirit.

I took my other hand and grabbed for my sword, but it was gone, lost somewhere in the fight. Harbinger's gray eyes shimmered with fear as he sensed his vulnerability. He threw himself backwards, escaping the current, and lay on the ground for several moments. Finally, he gathered the strength to get up and flee.

I reached up and shut the current off, before I managed to electrocute myself, and forced my body to get up. I removed my bomber jacket and t-shirt, mopping at my face with the once white, but now red, shirt.

Finally able to see, I made my way to Buddy, and realized I didn't have my knife. I looked around the floor for something sharp and remembered the closet. Going inside, I found a pair of wire cutters, returned to Buddy, and cut the straps.

I removed his gag as he got to a sitting position. He looked around for Harbinger.

"Is he gone?"

"Yes, at least I think so."

He looked me over.

"You look like crap!"

"Thanks, I feel like crap. Let's get out of here before he comes back for round two."

I retrieved my sword, helped him off the table, and we carried each other to the doorway. After a quick glance to make sure Big and Black was gone, we made our way to the street. Twenty minutes later, Buddy and I were separate rooms of the same hospital emergency ward.

EPILOGUE

The doctor came back into my room as I sat up on the bed.

"Lucky thing your nose broke."

"Really? Seems an odd sentence coming from a doctor; you need extra money for a new boat or something?"

"Funny. Actually, if your nose hadn't broke, the blow probably would have driven your nasal bone up into your brain, and we wouldn't be having this conversation."

"Doesn't seem like a pleasant experience, I'll take the broken nose."

He held an x-ray up to show me the fracture.

"I've laid a splint along here, which you need to leave on until the next time I see you."

"How long is that?"

"Couple weeks."

I didn't bother telling him I'd probably have it off in a couple days, no point in getting a lecture.

"Okay."

He handed me a mirror.

"Have you seen what you look like?"

"I'm not sure I want to."

I took the mirror anyway and checked out the damage. I had two giant black eyes coming on and a bandage covered most of my nose. I sounded funny from the gauze filling my nostrils.

"I took an x-ray of your arm as well. No break, and whoever doctored it, knew what they were doing."

"Thank you, Doctor."

We both turned to see my mother standing in the doorway.

"You're welcome. Can I ask who you are?"

"That's my mother. How did you get here?"

"By car."

"Very funny. You know what I mean."

"Amanda called me, since you neglected to."

She made an exaggerated pouty face.

"I was a little busy. Where's Mandy?"

"She's in with your friend Buddy. You look like a truck hit you and backed up to see what it ran over."

"That's pretty much how I feel."

She came over to take a closer look.

"What happened?"

"As I told the doctor, I was looking for Buddy downtown and this big guy jumped me."

She gave me a doubtful look.

"You seem to be having a lot of disagreements with strangers lately. Didn't you get in a fight when you injured your arm?"

I ignored the question.

"Am I ready to go, Doc?"

"I think so. There's a script for some pain meds. Pick it up when you sign your discharge papers."

"Okay, thanks Doc."

He left the room, and I started to get off the bed, when Mandy knocked.

"Can I come in?"

"Sure."

She came through the door and whistled.

"Wow! What's the other guy look like?"

"I don't know; he was running away the last time I saw him."

"Scared him?"

"I guess, but I wasn't exactly in the mood to chase him."

My mother slipped out of the room, hoping I wouldn't notice. I did, but I was glad. I knew Mandy had questions and I was going to have to be evasive. It's one thing to be evasive with a friend, but try doing it with your mother present, is impossible.

"Are you going to tell me what happened or are you going to clam up like your friend Buddy?"

"What did he say?"

"Nothing. I told him there was an open missing person case on him, and I needed answers to close it. He told me he was away."

She rolled her eyes and I had to smile. It hurt when my nose wrinkled.

Mandy brought her hand up to my face, lightly brushing my cheek, and staring into my eyes with those green diamonds of hers.

"You've got to be more careful. I'm not willing to lose you, and neither is your mother."

I was genuinely touched.

"Thanks, Mandy. I appreciate you saying so. I'll be more careful, I promise."

She gave me a sweet smile, and then turned all cop-like.

"So tell me what happened."

"I was downtown looking for Buddy when this big guy jumped me."

She gave me a suspicious squint of her eyes.

"So, two people have jumped you in less than a week? Seems kinda of odd, wouldn't you agree?"

I shrugged, which also hurt.

"Bad run of luck I guess."

"And where did you find Mr. Daniels?"

"I'd rather not say."

We were interrupted by another knock at the door.

"Can I come in?"

"Of course, Sarah."

When she came through the door, the relief of having her husband back was all over her face. At the same time, you could see the exhaustion from worrying about him.

She came over to the bed and Mandy excused herself.

Sarah gave me a warm smile.

"Thank you so much for bringing him home. He told me what happened, you're very brave."

"The Spirit granted me the courage. How is he doing?"

"The doctor said he's badly dehydrated, but otherwise unhurt. I think he told your cop friend he was away in the desert."

We both laughed, which hurt my face, but it was good to be happy again.

"Are you taking him home?"

"No. The doctor wants to keep him overnight and make sure his condition remains stable."

"Are you going to stay with him?"

"Yes. They're bringing in a bed for me."

She leaned over and kissed my cheek.

"Thanks again."

"You're welcome. Take care of him."

"I will."

She turned to leave the room, then stopped.

"I forgot. Buddy wanted me to give you this note."

She handed it to me and left the room.

I opened the note to find Buddy's chicken-scratch on a piece of hospital stationary.

Jack,

Harbinger ran tonight but he won't stay gone. Be cautious and ever-aware. He will try again.

Buddy

He was right, and I had no doubt it would be sooner rather than later.

I closed the note and realized I had someone who I needed to thank.

"Thank you Lord for helping me. Thank you Holy Spirit for helping me. With your strength, I survived. Amen."

****

A week later, I was paying my debts. Dinner for Mom and Mandy at Red Lobster.

Mandy was stunning in a long dress of blues and greens, highlighting her eyes and tan. Mom was also dressed up, and had spent the day at the beauty parlor before our dinner. She looked up from her dessert.

"How are Buddy and Sarah?"

"Good. Buddy's feeling a hundred percent again and back at his usual tasks. Sarah said she can finally breathe again."

I sat back in chair watched the two of them finish their Baked Alaska's. These are the two most important women in my life, both beautiful, and it was easy to realize how lucky I was.

My mother was there for me regardless of the circumstances, and she was willing to do it without getting answers to her questions.

And it didn't matter whether Mandy and I became romantically involved or not, I knew she had my back through good and bad, and that was something to treasure.

For probably the hundredth time in the last week, I looked towards heaven.

Thank you, Lord.

AUTHORS NOTE:

It is my sincere hope that you enjoyed reading this book as much as I enjoyed writing it. The idea quickly transferred to words on paper and my excitement grew with each page. I hope you feel your time spent reading was worth it.

If you would like to comment, my email is jdalglish7@gmail.com or you can visit my webpage at http://jcdalglish.webs.com. Keep up to date on Facebook at www.facebook.com/DetectiveJasonStrong

Thanks and God Bless,

John

I John 1:9

SPECIAL THANKS TO:

Beverly Dalglish – Cover
Samantha Gordon - Invisible Ink Editing

More by John C. Dalglish

THE CHASER CHRONICLES

CROSSOVER (#1)

JOURNEY (#2)

DESTINY (#3)

INNER DEMONS (#4)

DARK DAYS (#5)

DETECTIVE JASON STRONG SERIES

WHERE'S MY SON? (#1)

BLOODSTAIN (#2)

FOR MY BROTHER (#3)

SILENT JUSTICE (#4)

TIED TO MURDER (#5)

ONE OF THEIR OWN (#6)

DEATH STILL (#7)

LETHAL INJECTION (#8)

CRUEL DECEPTION (#9)

LET'S PLAY (#10)

HOSTAGE (#11)

Made in the USA
Coppell, TX
12 April 2021

53590943R00094